Wanderling's Choice

D.C. McLaughlin

Cover Design: H.A. Kennedy and Eren Fitzgerald
Author Photo: H.A. Kennedy

ISBN 13: 978-0-9895910-3-4

To Ellen. Never forget how to rope, ride or shoot.

PROLOGUE

This is what comes of wanting to have adventures! Her mind yelled at her while she ran.

Where is Falcon?

A myriad of frantic thoughts raced through her head as Rhiannon fled through the halls of the castle to the courtyard below in a flurry of silks and gems. But one thought was most important to her immediate circumstances.

She had to find her horse and get out of here.

Her words from the night before came back to haunt her.

"Am I permitted to ride my horse?" she had asked the king of the castle.

He had looked at her narrowly.

"Rhiannon, you no longer have any need of a horse. You are not permitted to leave the castle at any time, day or night. If you do, my servants have orders to kill you. Is that understood?"

Something hadn't felt quite right about the castle and now Rhi knew why.

This was no castle. It was her prison. A prison filled with servants with blank eyes, vacant of any soul whatsoever. A prison run by a jailer who called himself King Nazar.

More memories from the past few days came flooding into her mind. They did little to comfort her. They only made her feel more helpless and trapped by her situation.

Five young women had been led into the castle's sumptuous dining room where Rhi had been having dinner with King Nazar. *They were all beautiful. And they each had blank faces and the same soulless eyes as the other servants.*

"These are some of my most precious possessions" he had told her. "I found five pretty birds. They were each so lovely I could not let them fly free. Something bad might happen to them. So I caught them and put them here in my golden cage where they would be safe from all harm the cruel world might do them. I gave them every little thing a bird might want. I even asked each one to marry me. And still they were not happy."

His eyes shifted to meet Rhi's gaze.

"So I separated them from their souls. Now they do whatever I tell them to, whenever I tell them to do it. It doesn't matter now if they are happy or not. They're just birds, pretty to look at and play with but of no good use for anything really important other than my amusement."

His gaze held her eyes captive. They were cold and hard.

"Now I have found a sixth pretty bird to add to my collection."

Her blood ran cold remembering and an icy needle of dread went through her.

She had to find Falcon. She had to find her wonderful red stallion with the white mark on his forehead that looked like a pair of wings and get out of here. She didn't even care if she could locate the saddle and bridle. She just wanted to throw a leg over his back and fly out of this damned place that held her captive.

But the stable was empty. The stalls held nothing but cobwebs, moldy bedding and dusty tack. No horse had set foot here in quite a long time.

What has Nazar done to Falcon? Has he fed him to his pet dragon?

Her lungs burned and her feet ached. She wanted to be free.

She staggered to the courtyard and fell into a helpless heap of silver fabric and glittering gems.

This is what comes of wanting to have adventures, she thought again to herself. She had ridden Falcon mere days ago before Nazar had caught her and taken her hostage in this fine prison the rest of the world called a castle.

Up until this point in her life, her horse Falcon had been the center of her world. He had given her the life and freedom she so craved. She had never known that one ride on Falcon might be the last time she would ever see her dear horse. Now he was gone she didn't know where or how. She didn't even know if he was alive or dead. What had Nazar done to him?

She should have stayed home, she thought to herself. She should have stayed a simple unpretentious farmer's daughter, married the next door neighbor's son even though she only liked him, had a farm of their own and raised a bunch of kids. It would have been better. It would have been a sure thing. It would be doing what everyone around her had expected of her.

But no, she wanted to get a horse and wander the lands just the two of them having adventures and never ever *ever* getting married to anyone.

Now her only escape was to do what she had been trying to avoid all her life---getting married to a man she did not want.

Was it worth it? she wondered. *Was it really worth it at all?*

FALCON

"Rhi has turned into such a pretty young thing, hasn't she? I don't think there's another girl rich or poor around here half as beautiful as she. You must be so proud of her," their neighbor was saying. "She and Brody are going to make such pretty babies when they get married."

Rhiannon nearly dropped her basket of laundry. With an effort, she forced herself to continue with her chore, being careful to keep the sheets between them so no one would know she had been listening.

Brody was their neighbor's son down the lane. Rhi had known him since they both were toddlers. They had been playmates all through their childhood. She liked him plenty--- but not like that! He seemed more like one of her brothers. How could they possibly think they were lovers?

"Yes, they will, if he would just hurry up and ask her. She's getting rather old. Just imagine a seventeen-year old lass that's unmarried! Another couple of years and people will start calling her an old maid!" her mother replied and the two older women laughed like hens clucking over some juicy tidbit.

Rhi emptied her basket of laundry as quickly as she could then hurried around the corner of the chicken shed and sat down. She felt like an old horse who had galloped up a very steep hill. Her chest was tight and it was hard to breathe.

How dare they! was all she could think. She had no idea people thought of her in this manner. Here she was barely an adult and everyone already had her life all planned out for her.

The last thing Rhi wanted was to live her life according to everyone's preconceived expectations. No one had even asked her what she wanted.

She didn't even like Brody, not in the romantic sense at least. *How dare they!*

Rhi pulled herself to her feet and staggered over to the nearest paddock fence. She stared out at the scene before her. Bessie the family cow grazed contentedly on the long grass as it waved in the wind while the cow's calf gamboled beside her mother in the summer sun. Such a sight had always made Rhi feel free and happy before. Now she felt like the paddock rails were holding more than Bessie and the calf. The fence caged Rhi as well.

"I know what you're thinking!"

Rhi jumped in fright as her younger sister's voice piped up from her elbow.

"You're dreaming of Brody aren't you?"

Rhi's eyes narrowed and she frowned.

"Not even close," she growled in a low voice.

She spun on her heel and stalked away.

This was how it had all started. Her parents were planning on marrying her off to Brody. No one asked her, it was just assumed it would happen.

But Rhi wanted more, so much more than marriage and children.

Her mother had dowry money set aside for each of the girls when they got married. She had stashed it in a large tin kept high up in the eaves of the house with their names on each. The next morning Rhi awoke before the rest of her family stirred, took her dowry money and headed down the road away from the farm. Her family used this road to go to market.

But she wasn't going to market.

She instead went to the horse fair three miles in the other direction.

The horse fair happened every seven-day. It was held on the top of a hill called "Stallion's Bluff". People came from far and wide to buy and sell horses of all sizes and types. Rhi had loved coming here as a child.

But that was a long time ago. And Rhi knew the difference now between a cart horse, a plow horse, a work horse and a merchant, or messenger horse. She could also tell the difference between a good buy and a slick deal.

Rhi walked through the gates and took a moment to catch her breath and take in the sights. There were horses everywhere and people wheeling and dealing. The air was thick with the smell of manure and fresh hay and the squeals and neighs of frightened or excited horses.

The first thing Rhi noticed wasn't a particular horse but a man, a small, thin man leaning up against a carriage. He was dressed all in brown and green and wore a great, floppy hat on his head. His face was weather-beaten and lined so his age was difficult to guess. He seemed to be much older than Rhi. He smiled at her from a mouth a bit too wide and his eyes looked old and sad.

His sad eyes sparkled at her. Sweeping his great hat off his head, he bowed and nodded a greeting to her.

A man then led two great dray horses between them and when Rhi looked again, he was gone from sight as if he had never been.

'*Well that was odd*,' she thought to herself, then shook the memory out of her head. In the next moment she had forgotten all about it.

She continued on in her search.

It seemed to Rhi she must have spoken to every horse dealer there. They all knew of her family and tried to sell her old, plow horses no matter how much she told them she didn't want a work horse.

Frustrated and steamed, because the day had turned hot, she sat down on a stump in the sun since all the shade was taken, to eat her meager lunch. Suddenly her bench was shielded by a welcoming, cool shadow.

She looked up to see the man who had first nodded to her. He had removed his great, floppy hat and was holding it out to shade her, revealing his lank, blonde hair.

"Pardon me, lass, but it is too hot a day for a miss as pretty as you to eat in the sun," he said.

His accent was one she had never heard before.

"The horses need the shade more. But thank I you for your kind offer," she replied.

"You did not bring anything to drink?" he asked.

"No," she laughed. "I remembered food but forgot drink. How silly of me!"

He smiled and held out a small flask.

"It's just water. I do not drink alcohol. People tend to do stupid things when they drink."

Rhi hesitated. He was a stranger and a horse dealer. They had a murky reputation.

But it was so hot!

She muttered her thanks and took a shy swig from the stranger's flask. It was simply water and nothing more. But it was ice cold. She took a more daring gulp.

The stranger pulled up another log to sit beside her.

"How is your search for that perfect horse going?" he inquired pleasantly.

With a roll of her eyes she told him "They all want to sell me cart and plow horses!"

He laughed in sympathy.

"Too many dealers here think that a pretty face such as yours cannot possibly be a good judge of horse flesh."

"I don't want the perfect horse, just a good using horse."

"Hmmm," he nodded. "And just what is your definition of 'a good using horse'?"

Rhi sighed and thought a bit.

"Well, nothing so big that I need a ladder to get on but nothing too short...*not* a plow horse, or a cart horse or a work horse!'

"Ahhh!" he breathed in comprehension. "You want a riding horse!"

"Yes!" Rhi agreed. "I don't care about the color, although something not so fancy as it attracts enough attention to get stolen but something not downright ugly would be good. Something not too flighty with a good, smart mind, something with a good turn of speed, something tough and hardy for rough terrain and weather, something that can get by on little food and without shoes, something like a good merchant or messenger horse, maybe even a light warhorse whose brain hasn't been ruined by his experience. You know, a good using horse."

The man laughed at her.

"Well, you don't want much, do you, lass? Just the perfect horse."

Rhi's face fell. She felt like she had just been slapped.

"No, no! Don't misunderstand me. I'm not laughing at you. It just so happens I have six horses and one particularly special one that might fit the description."

Rhi looked at him with hope and then suspicion.

"Lass, if I was trying to hustle you, that flask would not have mere water in it."

Rhi chewed her last bite of bread slowly and thoughtfully as she looked him up and down.

"Finish your meal and I will show you my stock."

She wrapped up the remainders of her meal and replaced them in her satchel and got to her feet.

"But I think I've seen every horse on Stallion's Bluff," Rhi said.

"Oh but you haven't seen my stock," he assured her. "I keep them off the bluff in a private grove until I think I have a potential buyer. Just follow me!"

Her inner senses began to whisper a warning in her ear. He wanted her to follow him off the bluff, far from other people, to a secluded area? What about this sounded trustworthy?

But follow him she did, off the bluff, onto the wooded hillside, into a small private glen. She followed at a distance, making sure she had enough space between them if she needed to make a quick retreat.

They rounded a corner of the wood and came to a small paddock.

"Here they are, my pretties, my beauties. Aren't they wonderful?"

Rhi came to a sudden stop and her jaw dropped.

Six of the loveliest horses she had ever clapped eyes on stood in the paddock. They were all groomed within an inch of their lives and their coats gleamed like metal. Their legs were clean and blemish free, their bare hooves solid and healthy, their well chiseled faces looked at her with a quiet intelligence.

"They're....they're...beautiful!" she gasped.

"Of course they are. I know my horseflesh and I take good care of them. But these horses are not for you."

She had to give it a moment to let the words sink in before she realized she had lost sight of the strange little thin man.

"Here is you perfect horse, lass." He spoke softly and he was suddenly standing right beside her.

He held the reins of a magnificent, coppery chestnut stallion. His mane was long, thick and silky, his coat was soft as down and shiny as a penny. The eyes which met hers were intelligent and soulful. When Rhi touched his face, he lowered his head and breathed softly into her hands. He snorted and shook his head, revealing a small white mark on his forehead which looked like wings.

"I've re-adjusted the stirrups. They should be the right length for your legs. Why don't you take him for a test ride, lass?"

Almost in a dream, Rhi found herself putting a foot in the stirrup and bounding unaided into the saddle. The stallion waited until she settled herself and her skirts around his sides. Then he breathed softly and began to move as if she had cued him with her mind.

His walking steps were confident and smooth making her sit deep into the saddle. He arched his neck proudly and slid into an effortless trot. They trotted an elegant figure eight formation.

She almost startled when she heard the man call out to her, "The lassie has a good scat."

They did two more figure eights and the stallion did just as he was bid.

"Does he move like a plow horse?"

She gave a trembling giggle.

"Heavens no!"

She chanced a look up to the horse dealer. He was beaming at her.

"Why don't you see what a real gallop feels like?"

She could feel the stallion underneath her hesitate just as she was hesitating. Then he pulled gently, quietly on the reins as if to say *Please? May I?*

She turned him to face the steep slope of the bluff, leant forward over his neck, lessened her grip on the reins. At the same time she hissed in his ear and gave his sides a gentle rap with her heels.

And the stallion exploded underneath her! With a bellow and a leap, his great hooves attacked the earth of the hill. Rhi was startled for just a moment. She found his great lunge hadn't dislodged her and they were still together, she clung like a tick and felt the power roll out of him from beneath her. He was strong and fast, faster than any horse she had ever thrown a leg over, in his prime and full of himself. And yet he was still right there with her. He hadn't left her behind.

What a horse!

He slowed his mad dash the minute she thought about it and easily came back to a slower pace.

Rhi loved this horse! And she felt he liked her and would have done anything to please her. She had to have him. But she was now sure she didn't have enough money to purchase him. Not on a farmer's daughter's dowry!

She chewed her lip as she thought this.

The horse dealer was grinning ear to ear as she rode up to him.

"Well, that was certainly a sight, and no mistake. You move as one! He is the perfect mount for you."

Rhi nodded and grudgingly pulled out her small purse which she was now sure held not enough coin to purchase such an animal.

"How much?" she muttered.

For the first time, he touched her. The little man grabbed her hand to stop her.

"No! This horse is not for sale for gold."

Rhi gave him a confused look. What racket was he trying to pull?

"Yes, you can buy this horse. But not for money."

His hand had released hers and was now resting on the skirts over her leg.

Rhi's eyes flew wide as the other option became clear to her.

It seemed to dawn on the horse trader as well because suddenly he let go of her and holding both hands up in the air, he backed away from both horse and rider.

"Now don't mistake me, lass. I never meant...*THAT*!"

Rhi's frown deepened.

"Then what do you mean? Speak plainly! So far you've only spoken in riddles."

He laughed and waggled his head.

"Yes, I can see where you came up with the idea."

He sighed heavily.

"It's like this. I'm not a horse trader. I'm a horse matcher. I match the correct horse with the correct person. I do not accept money for this. I accept tokens."

Rhi pursed her lips.

"Tokens. What sort of tokens?"

"Name him. This horse has had other riders and other names. They all were wrong. Find the correct name for this animal and you will prove to me you belong together."

This was the oddest arrangement that Rhi had ever heard of! And yet it made sense to her.

So she thought. She thought about the mad dash up the hill and how perfectly suited they seemed to be for each other. She thought about how beautiful he was and how he seemed to fly. She thought about the white marking on his head.

She looked up into the sky.

A bird was circling them slowly overhead. It cried out, the keen of a bird of prey. It flapped its wings and as the wings fluttered, a single feather was dislodged and drifted, spinning in slow spirals to earth. Without thinking Rhi positioned the horse underneath the fluttering feather. She caught it and examined it closely. It was the same glossy red color as her horse.

"Falcon." She whispered at first and then spoke louder. "His name is Falcon."

The man smiled, nodded and walked up to her. Silently he removed the feather from her hands. He stroked the feather lovingly, smoothing down its parted sections.

"We have an accord. The stallion is yours, milady. His name is Falcon."

He placed the feather in his great floppy hat, graced her with another sweep and bow and suddenly he was gone. He just disappeared right before her eyes. So did his paddock and the other six horses, again as if they had never been.

But the great red chestnut stallion Falcon was still beneath her.

Rhi had found her horse.

***

Rhi and Falcon cantered the rest of the day and most of the night. She didn't care where she was heading. She just picked a direction the road seemed to be going in and took it. She rode until her seat grew sore and Falcon grew damp underneath her. Then she remembered she better take care of her horse and slowed him to a walk. They walked for three miles, until Falcon had stopped panting and the sweat had dried on him.

Her head began to nod. She then decided she had better rest both of them. But she didn't want to bed down right at the side of the road. She pushed steadily onward until she heard a stream bordering their way. Her tired eyes searched for a proper place and soon she found a small clearing on the other side of the stream.

She guided Falcon off the road, down the embankment and across the stream. Wearily she dismounted and unsaddled Falcon. She took off her shoes and led him to the middle of the stream. As he drank his fill she splashed his sides where the sweat had dried and scrubbed the crunchy areas with her fingers. The stream water was cold from ice melt from the nearby mountains but the night was warm. She had no fear of shocking his muscles.

She should have made a fire and cooked some food. But she was too tired. She only had the energy to shake out her blanket, and using the saddle as a pillow, she lay down on the thick grass with Falcon grazing nearby. Nighttime was just melting into morning. Dawn was tinging the horizon with orange. She gave a heavy sigh and closed her eyes, surrendered to sleep.

She awoke to the sound of a crackling fire and the aroma of cooking meat. Her stomach yowled in hunger. She groaned and stretched. Her muscles complained at her bad choice of a bed. Her neck was stiff and her legs and rump sore from the ride the day before. She rose to her elbows and looked about wildly for her horse. Wouldn't it just be perfect if he had wandered off during the night!

But Falcon was there beside her, his belly full of grass, swishing the flies away with his heavy tail. He looked at her then shook his head and snorted as if to say, *You sleep too much*, and he resumed grazing. The entire clearing had been cropped close of all its grass, except for the patch where she was sleeping.

She stiffly rolled over and eyeballed the fire warily. Someone had made it a good while ago because there was already a thick bed of orange coals. It was ringed in river stones and an iron spit had been erected over it upon which a butchered rabbit had been skewered.

She looked about suspiciously but there was no one around. The smell of the roasting meat made her mouth water. She removed the skewered rabbit and cautiously tasted it. Somebody had taken their time preparing it. It was seasoned to perfection and cooked thoroughly and evenly. She devoured it hungrily as if it was the best rabbit she had ever tasted.

When there was nothing left but bones, she went to the stream and washed her hands and face thoroughly with the little pat of lard soap she had thought to bring with her. This done, she brushed out her long, russet locks. She returned to the fire and picked up her saddlebags. Rhi rummaged through them, checked her gear and re-arranged things. She had everything pulled out but something still rattled about inside the left pouch. She turned it upside down and shook it forcefully.

A flash of silver and white fell out attached to a leather cord.

She picked it up and examined it more closely.

It was a silver medallion. There was an inscription on the back which she could not make out. Unlike most farmers' daughters, Rhi could read but she couldn't read this. The inscription seemed to dance and flutter like bright sunlight on ripples of water in a clear pool. It dazzled and confused her eyes so much she wasn't sure what she was looking at.

She flipped the medallion over in her hands. The front face held the delicate etching of a feather, nothing more, just a white feather on a disc of silver flashing in the noonday sun. She had never seen such a token before and had no idea what it stood for or what it symbolized.

"Falcon tells me you rode him hard," a heavily accented voice said to her from across the glade.

She gasped, startled and spun about.

The horse dealer stood there stroking the nose of the red chestnut tenderly.

"He also said you took very good care of him when you stopped before you saw to your own needs."

The little, thin, man with the sad eyes and the floppy hat came over to sit beside her on a fallen log.

"Are you following me?" Rhi said.

He smiled, took off his hat and laid it on his knee.

"No my dear. The path you have chosen just happens to be the same way I am going. Simple coincidence and nothing more. You certainly don't need me to hold your hand along the way."

"And you made the roast rabbit?" she asked.

He nodded. "Did you enjoy my cooking?"

"Yes, I did. I guess I should have saved you some."

He laughed and waved her off.

"Don't worry. I have already eaten. But after a hard ride, I decided you needed some meat in your diet."

Rhi stabbed the campfire coals thoughtfully. She wasn't sure she wanted company right now especially with the man who had sold her Falcon. It felt awkward somehow, like he was checking up on her and making sure she took good care of the horse. Would he renege on the sale if he thought she didn't treat Falcon right?

"So now you speak to horses? How is that possible?" she asked.

He too picked up a stick and began to absently poke at the fire.

"There's an old story in my family that many generations ago, an elf married into my clan. Now I'm not sure whether the elf was male or female or even if the story is true. But members of my family find it very easy to understand and be understood by animals. When I found out I had some sort of power of communication with horses, I stopped selling them and started matching them to the correct rider. It has been a much more fulfilling career than the one I had before."

Rhi listened to his explanation carefully but was still doubtful.

"Whether or not it's a better, more honest way of making a living, you still need money sometimes. I mean, I don't think you make your own clothes, except for that strange hat of yours. What do you do when you really need gold to buy something with?"

"Oh, I have no problem getting money when I need it. You see, Rumplestiltskin is my uncle."

Rhi stared at him.

"You are the oddest man I have ever met!"

And his already wide mouth split even wider in mirth.

"Was any of that gibberish true?"

He sniffed and shook his head.

"I don't really care whether you think it's true or not, lass. It makes for a good story, does it not?"

Rhi sniffed.

"You know you seem very eager to have me believe you are an honest person in a dishonest world. But I don't think you're beyond a little petty theft now and then."

He *tssked* at her as if disappointed.

"My dear you wound me deeply!" he said. His words were pained but his expression was very amused. "Now what have I done to make you think I'm a thief?"

"I think you stole the tack Falcon came with."

He gasped dramatically.

"I certainly did not!"

Rhi just waggled a scolding finger at him.

"Oh! But I think you did!"

He shook his head in denial.

"Prove it, lass!"

Rhi smiled.

"Fine! Then where did this come from?"

She held aloft the medallion on the leather cord.

Suddenly the man beside her wasn't teasing anymore. His expression was one of true shock, a sheep cornered by the clever sheepdog.

"Where did you find that?"

"In one of the saddlebags, as if you didn't know. Tell me you did not steal it."

He took a deep breath and looked her full in the eye. "I did not steal it."

Rhi just held his gaze for a long moment.

"But you recognize it, don't you? It has an inscription on the back but I can't read it. What does it say?"

He swallowed with difficulty and slowly took it from her. He turned it over and over in his hands.

"It's in an ancient tongue no one can now read."

He stood up and slowly walked around behind her. She saw the medallion flash as he held it before her face momentarily and then lowered it to rest against the skin of her throat. She felt him begin to tie it about her neck and without thinking, held her long locks out of the way.

"It found you and therefore it now belongs to you. Wear it and it will protect you in your darkest hours on the road. This is all I am permitted to tell you at this time. I give you my word on this, Rhiannon."

Rhi sat up straight as she realized something.

"How do you know my name?"

He would not reply. Yet still she could feel him standing behind her.

"How can I believe the word of a man whose name I don't even know?"

She felt rather than saw him smile.

He laid his hands very gently and lightly on her shoulders.

"My name is Shayne. Remember that. Shayne."

And then he let go of her.

Rhi spun about.

He was gone. She was alone once again.

***

The next day Rhi started her new life, a life of her choosing. All she wanted was to live her life her way, to be the master of her own future. This was why she had run away from the farm, her family and everything she had ever known. For several years she wandered the surrounding lands during the spring and summer. During the cold winters she found someone to shelter her until the spring thaw. The moment the ground had softened and the weather warmed she and Falcon would be off again wandering the lands. Nothing was certain. She had no idea where she would sleep from one day to the next or where her next meal would come from. And Rhi found she liked it that way. No one told her what to do. No one expected her to live or behave a certain way. Only the weather, terrain and nature ruled her. She was completely free from anyone's expectation but her own.

Sometimes she would run into Shayne. She might only catch a glimpse of him from a distance and they would smile and wave to each other, or they might share a meal and catch up on the goings on in each other's lives. He seemed to be particularly pleased with the way she had chosen to live her life, free and independent.

So her life continued with few bumps in the road. Until the day when she decided to attend one particular horse fair.

the horse thieves

It seemed like just another horse fair. It was in a new land they had never visited before at the foot of a chain of mountains. The people there had strange accents and ways. They seemed less likely to be friendly to strangers, especially a woman stranger, traveling alone, dressed in men's attire. Rhi liked the countryside but not the people. She decided to find out news in the area from this horse fair and then move on to someplace with friendlier, less taciturn inhabitants.

She caught a glimpse of Shayne at this fair way off in the distance but he didn't see her. She decided to look him up later if the people here continued to frustrate her with their ways.

And frustrate her they did. Nobody seemed willing to talk to her except other women and even the other women looked askance at her. They were polite enough but the body language they gave off seemed to say, "What are you doing here dressed like that?"

She left Falcon tied to a fence rail to go buy a small meal from one of the food vendors. When she returned she found two very scruffy, greasy looking men taking a great interest in Falcon. And Falcon seemed somewhat upset at their close proximity. He didn't enjoy their attention.

"Excuse me, can I help you?' she said. The tone of voice which came out of her mouth surprised her. She didn't mean to speak in such an irritated way.

One man glanced at her as if she was a piece of furniture.

"Go get your man. We need to speak to the owner of this horse."

Rhi stood up straight and tall.

"I have no man. And the horse belongs to me."

This response served to get their full attention focused now on her. She felt like Falcon a moment before; like a piece of meat being leered at by a hungry person covered in slime.

Rhi slipped one of her hands under her satchel and began to reach for the short sword concealed underneath the cloak.

One of the men shook his head and muttered not so quietly, "What's the world coming to when a no-account woman can own a horse, especially a good one and a stallion at that?"

Rhi felt her face grow hot and she stiffened inwardly.

"How much?" the other man said speaking to her as if he expected her not to understand the concept.

"Not for sale," she shot back clearly.

They laughed as if she had made a bad joke.

"C'mon, biddy. Everything has its price," he said to her and looked her up and down lecherously.

She knew exactly what he meant and she did not appreciate being called 'biddy'.

"Not him," she insisted.

"Then whaddya bring him to a horse fair if you didn't plan on selling' im?" grumbled the other man tartly.

Rhi cleared her throat.

"Sir, if you have a goodly mare you'd like to breed to him, then we can talk business. If not, then we have no business to discuss."

Before they could reply to this, she whistled. Falcon untied himself from the slip-knot she had secured him to the post with and trotted eagerly over to her.

She took hold of the rope, nodded to them both and wished them a good day, turned and left. She wanted to swing up on Falcon's back and gallop away as fast as he could run. But she also didn't want to make a scene.

She could feel their eyes boring into her back as she walked away.

She walked Falcon into the center of a big throng of people and horses just to get him out of their sight. Normally Falcon would get all excited and start dancing and talking to all the other strange horses. But this time he was quiet and steady by her side.

Falcon suddenly stopped and snorted in friendly greeting at a man who blocked their path.

"Shayne!" Rhi breathed a huge sigh of relief.

Shayne had a worried look on his face.

"What are you doing here, Rhi?" he said to her.

Rhi was startled at his tone of voice. He almost seemed angry with her.

"This is no horse fair you and Falcon should attend. There are some very unsavory individuals here."

Rhi rolled her eyes and shrugged.

"Too late! I already bumped into two prime examples," she replied.

Shayne took hold of her shoulder and stepped closer to whisper quietly to her.

"They do not deal well with women in this province, especially a business woman like yourself. What you're doing here is almost looked on as a crime. You need to leave now. Go far and fast before one of these rude brutes decides to teach you his lesson of respect. I will guard your departure."

He handed her Falcon's tack and nodded. She passed Shayne the lead rope and he held Falcon as she saddled and bridled him as quickly as she was able to. He passed her the halter and lead rope and she stuffed them in her saddlebags. She slid him a quick glance. Shayne smiled, nodded again and gave her shoulder an encouraging squeeze. Even though she did not need his help to mount Falcon, he boosted her on.

As she gathered up the reins, he touched her arm. She looked down at him.

"The medallion…it looks beautiful on you, by the way," he said as he gazed up at her sitting in the saddle. The bright noonday sun erased some of the lines of worry from his face.

Once again she wondered what the significance of the silver disc was and why he wouldn't tell her its meaning.

Then she noticed the red feather she had given him years ago was no longer in his floppy hat. Its shaft had been dipped in metal and it now swung from a silver chain around his neck, barely hidden by his shirt.

This made her pause. It was just a mere falcon's feather, simple, but obviously very special to him.

Before she could think more on this, he clapped Falcon on the rump and they galloped away, out of the throng of people, out of the horse fair gates away from the festival.

Many eyes took note of their departure.

***

Rhi rode Falcon hard and fast all the day. When dusk came, she took him off the roads and into the woodlands. She rode for about an hour after sunset to find a well-hidden place to make camp. She left the bridle and saddle on Falcon but loosened the girth and removed her bags. She decided against a fire and ate a cold meal instead.

She was just about to roll herself into her blankets when there came the snapping sound of something large stepping on brittle branches. Falcon started and his body language changed. He was no longer a horse relaxing after a hard day's ride. He was all tense and alert, his muscles twitching, ears poised forward in the direction of the sound.

Rhi too came to life. Her heart started to race. Was it a wild animal or worse? Her eyes searched the dark underbrush. But she saw nothing.

Then a small white pouch sailed out of the woods and hit Falcon on the flank. It immediately exploded into a white powder. Falcon jumped and reared in fright with a small squeal. In his excitement, he spun into the white cloud which was quickly rising from the ground. He suddenly staggered as if he was drunk and groaned.

Rhi knew exactly what had happened. Her horse was being drugged!

She lunged for her pack and grabbed for the short sword at her side in the same moment. But a rough hand clutched hers before she could reach it and whipped her around to face her attacker.

Her frightened eyes stared into the night-darkened face of one of the horse traders she had run afoul of earlier in the day.

He smiled widely at her. His breath had an awful stench and most of his front teeth were missing.

Then his fist, hard as a brick, crashed into her face and the world went black.

***

Rhi woke up to grass beneath her. Her whole face was swollen, hot and throbbing and she couldn't open her right eye. She tried to carefully assess her surroundings.

A large fire had been built in the clearing. Falcon lay just beyond her on the ground. His hooves were bound tight and his sides were heaving so she knew he was still alive.

There was a small huddle of rawboned, wormy looking horses tied to a picket line off in the shadows. They stood with their heads down and eyes closed, without grazing, as if they did not care what happened to them anymore. But their hooves flashed and glittered strangely in the dark of the night.

Rhi tried to move her head without being seen and looked toward the campfire. Five large, man shapes were gathered across from her, on the other side of the flames. They were drinking and laughing and poking through her belongings in the saddlebags.

"How did this broad get so much money?" one said in an alcohol slurred voice.

"Must've stolen it," coughed another. "Nice haul though. We got ourselves a heavy pouch of gold, a fine sword *and* a good stallion to make a pretty penny off of. Bonuses all around. Drink up, boys!"

Another man belched rudely.

"But whadda we do wif her?"

"Waddaya mean?"

"I mean we came to steal a horse. She was never part of the bargain."

Another one snorted and sputtered into his mug.

"Didn't you hear the boss? Bonuses all around! She's a bonus!"

The biggest man shape shrugged and waved as if it made no difference to him.

"I don't care what you do with her! Sell her as a slave in the next town, tenderize her a bit, take turns having fun with her and then dump her body in the river, whatever. I'm sure you'll think of something."

Rhi felt the breath in her throat turn icy.

"She said she has no man. That means no one is looking for her."

Another one guffawed as he slugged his drink, "She's not royalty and that's certain. So no good asking for a ransom."

The smaller man coughed.

"You ever heard of someone asking for a reward for a simple peasant lass? No one will miss her."

They all laughed as one.

"I guess that means we can all line up for a ride then!"

Rhi's heart was pounding in terror by now.

"Hey! She's moving! She's waking up."

They all looked in her direction. Rhi tried not to whimper in fear.

"I'll fix that!" grumbled the first one and before any of his drunken fellows could stop him, he stooped and threw a hot rock from the fire at Rhi. She rolled away but it clocked her across the top of her head, etching a long, bloody, gash into her scalp.

She moaned in pain and fought the wave of unconsciousness which threatened to envelop her again. She tried to crawl away into the darkness.

Running footsteps caught up with her and she was suddenly pinned to the ground by a hobnailed boot.

"Don't kill her!" shouted one. "I like it when they scream."

Rhi moaned in hopelessness. Without knowing how, the fingers of her right hand found the silver medallion which still dangled around her throat.

"Shayne, help me," she whispered without even thinking.

She prayed this nightmare would just go away.

And then she got her wish.

There was sudden flash of brilliant, white light.

The hard boot seemed to be knocked off her back. The man above her shrieked in surprise and pain. Blood splashed Rhi in the face and fell like rain about her. And then with a hard thud, he was lying on the ground next to Rhi. His face was inches from hers, his wide, frightened eyes frozen open. There was a line of blood across his throat and Rhi could see his cut windpipe clearly exposed.

He was dead.

She squeaked in surprise and rolled onto her back.

"Who's next?" Shayne dared them.

Rhi didn't know who was more surprised, the robbers or her.

Shayne stood between the thieves and her. He looked different. He was no taller but had adopted the warrior's stance, feet positioned in a lunge, short sword held out in front of him. His expression was hard and cold as ice. He looked quite fearsome.

The robbers were startled but recovered fast. They exchanged looks among themselves and Rhi could tell they were going to rush him all at once and try to overwhelm him.

Shayne just smiled and beckoned them to try and do so with his free hand.

The thieves roared as one and charged him. Shayne sidestepped the first one easily, ducked and tripped the second, pushed the third one into the fire and kicked hot coals into the face of another. While two were busy screaming from the fire's effects, he spun smoothly on his heel and engaged the other two.

The one thief danced easily about him and Rhi thought for a minute Shayne would be skewered. But his reactions were smoother and faster than the robber. He sidestepped the stab and slashed his sword across the robber's wrist making him drop the sword. Shayne caught it by the hilt before the weapon had a chance to revolve once in its plummet to earth and with his own sword, Shayne slashed the side of the robber's neck. A well-placed kick to the chest knocked the fatally wounded man out of the way and Shayne turned his attention to the next thief. The other man tried to dodge Shayne's attack but was too drunk with alcohol and stumbled. Shayne spun the hilt of the sword around in his fingers and stabbed him once in the chest, in and out.

He then turned to the two burned robbers.

The one who got hot coals in the face rushed at him, shouting and slashing in wild, blind motions. Shayne stabbed him in the side mortally wounding him as he went crashing by.

The last one who got hot coals in the chest, grabbed a handful of them in his glove and threw the burning embers at Shayne. It was a desperate action meant to buy him time and Shayne knew it. He dodged the toss easily. But then the man crashed into him before he could bring his swords up to bear and with a grunt and a thud they fell tumbling to earth. Shayne dropped one of his swords. Each had hold of the other's hands and they rolled about, trying to out-grapple the other.

Rhi crawled to her hands and knees as they rolled about and painfully scrambled to where they had emptied her saddlebags. She took back her sword and clutching it to her chest protectively, turned back to the fight. Shayne and the robber were still wrestling on the ground. They scrambled and fought to break each other's hold.

Their kicking struggle rolled them close to Rhi. But both were so involved in the fight, they didn't see her. Rhi noticed the thief was a lot bigger than Shayne.

Another twist and grunt and they bumped closer to her. Rhi saw an opening and dove in with her sword. She felt the blade cut smoothly through flesh, scrape bone and impale organs. There was a hideous scream and a shudder. Rhi felt the man scream through the sword in her hand. She jerked the sword free and dropped it.

Both men stopped moving. A deathly silence now blanketed the clearing broken only by the cracks and pops from the fire.

Rhi just tried to catch her breath for a moment. A horrible thought occurred to her. What if, in stabbing her captor, she had made a mistake and accidentally killed Shayne?

"Shayne?" she called fearfully. "Shayne!"

An arm flopped out from under the two men and its fingers reached for her. Shayne rolled his head over to look at her. He seemed very winded and struggled to catch his breath.

"Still alive," he gasped.

With a sob of relief, Rhi grabbed his one hand with both of hers and clung tight.

Then she fainted.

Shayne

When she awoke, she was propped up in a sitting position against a rock and Shayne was stitching her scalp closed.

"You had to wake up now! I'm almost done," he muttered.

Rhi whimpered and tried to lie very still. It was a very strange feeling as the needle went through her skin and the jagged edges were pulled closed. Her scalp was pouring blood as he finished. Luckily he only had two more stitches to do. This done, he produced a bowl of warm water and some clean rags and began to carefully wash the blood from her face. His touch was very gentle. In spite of this she still gasped in pain.

"I'm sorry," he consoled. "I'm doing my best not to hurt you. You've lost a lot of blood. It's the nature of head wounds."

"How did they find me?" she finally managed to ask.

"They had help, magical help," he told her. "Their horses had enchanted horseshoes that allowed them to travel faster than any normal horse. They also had a gem which allowed them to track anybody they wanted to. They were bound to find you. If I had known this at the horse fair, I would have never left your side."

He finished cleaning her face and turned his inspection to her swollen eye.

"Did they hurt you in any other way? I mean….like…"

She didn't want to hear him say the word "rape" to her.

"No," she answered quickly. "But they were about to."

She dropped the gaze of her one good eye to the ground.

"I feel stupid that you had to come and save me. I should have never gotten into this situation in the first place."

Shayne had rescued her. This meant Rhi had been put into a predicament that made her helpless. And she hated being helpless!

"Hush! The important thing is that I got there before anything really horrible happened to you. You were very lucky, my dear."

He began to clean up the medical supplies.

Rhi's face was beginning to throb and talking hurt because it pulled on her swollen mouth.

"There's one thing I don't understand though," Shayne said thoughtfully.

"Mmm. What?" Rhi hoped that it wouldn't be a long answer.

Shayne went to the edge of the campsite and dumped out the bloody water.

"You called for a hero to come and rescue you. You could have called for anyone…a knight in armor, a constable, your true love. Instead you called for me. Why me?"

Rhi sighed. All right! That's the way he wanted it, a long answer.

"I have no true love," she insisted.

He looked her straight in the face.

"I guess I figured if I ever needed rescuing….I'd want you to do it. Just you. No one else." She gave a big sigh.

Shayne nodded. "Okay," he said slowly, "But why me?"

"Because you're the only one in this crazy world I trust."

He just looked at her for a long moment. "You trust a horse trader?" he said quietly.

She sniffed and winced in pain at the motion.

"You're not a horse trader!" she insisted with some heat. "You're not like any horse trader I've ever met before. There's a touch of magic about you, that much is obvious. Who or what you are I don't know. But not a horse trader!"

Shayne was very quiet. He went to his bags and produced what looked like a wineskin. He returned to her side and handed it to her.

"It's not water," he told her. "Take a couple swigs of this. It will help you heal and take care of some of the pain."

She did as he bid. The liquid burned like hot fire going down her throat.

"You're too hurt to travel much," he continued. "We'll stay here until you've healed up. It's safe enough here now."

She almost laughed.

"You're to be my nurse?"

Shayne smiled. It was an easy, true smile. "I have the time. And I don't mind," he replied.

She wondered if she had broken down enough defenses to get him to talk. "Shayne, will you ever tell me your story, your *real* story?"

He had stood up and gone to replace the wineskin. "Maybe someday."

Rhi shrugged. "We have plenty of time now."

He kept his back turned to her, hiding his face. She felt he had left her somehow. His mind was someplace far, far away.

"It is not a pleasant tale," he said quietly. For a moment she thought he would tell her.

"And it pains me to relive it. So no, not now. But someday maybe."

He replaced his gear and returned to sit beside her. His expression was lighter and more carefree than a moment ago.

Rhi considered him for a long minute. The firelight flashed off the setting on the feather he wore about his neck.

"The feather I gave you, why did you keep it?" she asked.

He shrugged as if the answer should be obvious to her. "Because you gave it to me."

She shook her head as much as she was able to. "No, that's not it. It's just a feather. It's not a ring or a jewel or a magic charm. Just a feather. What's so important about it?"

He gave a small smile. "My dear, do you realize how many pretty, young, women give me nice things?"

Again she shook her head.

"No one. Just you. Therefore it is important to me. And yes, it is magic. To me, no one else. There's a lot of magic in little things."

This only served to confuse her more.

He gave her an even wider, more maddening smile. "Oh by the way, the potion I made you drink? It also makes you sleep."

As he said this, her eyelids drooped, her head nodded and rolled to the side and she fell into a deep slumber.

Shayne gently eased her off of the rock and laid her down flat on the ground. He arranged the goatskin saddle-pad for a pillow underneath her head and tucked in the blankets. Then he just sat there on the grass next to her and looked at her for a long while. Shayne picked up her hand and stroked it affectionately.

"I wonder…are you the one?" he whispered.

He stroked the uninjured side of her face once.

"I want you to be the one."

He toyed with the feather he wore about his neck. He then picked up the small, silver medallion she wore. He flipped it over and read the inscription. His expression was blank.

"Why have you wormed your way into my heart, little lass, when no other woman has?"

He heaved a heavy sigh, one full of memories and disappointments, dreams and despair. He released her hand and tucked the covers in about her.

Then he peered closely into her sleeping face.

"Save me, Rhiannon," he spoke softly to her.

Shayne bent low and kissed her tenderly on the forehead.

He then returned to his own bedroll across the campfire and closer to the horses.

***

Rhi slept long and hard thanks to the effects of the potion. She awoke late in the day when the sun had dipped low on the horizon. She saw no sign of Shayne.

She sat up and looked about. Somehow it didn't feel like he had left her. The fire was blazing and an iron pot has been set to boil over it. Falcon had been released from his bonds and looked much better, if somewhat subdued in disposition. The robber's horses looked like they were coming back to life again. They were grazing contentedly on their picket line.

Slowly, carefully, Rhi got to her feet. Her head throbbed a little but it was nothing like the day before. The swelling over her eye was going down and she could actually see some out of it. She bet it looked a sight! Rhi was glad she didn't have a mirror.

Where HAS Shayne gone? she wondered.

She wandered about the campsite a bit looking for him. She heard the trickle of a stream and followed the sound. And there she found Shayne.

He was barefoot, stripped to his waist and standing knee deep in the stream. His upper half was covered in dirt.

She knew she shouldn't have spied on him. But she watched anyway as he scrubbed the dirt from his arms and chest. He splashed himself liberally with the icy water then dunked his head and shook it through his hair. He flung back his hair and straightened up. She watched the water rain off of him and the sun glisten on his wet skin.

He turned around and saw her.

"How long have you been standing there?"

She blushed, embarrassed and turned away. She didn't answer. She just made her way back to the camp. She heard him mutter behind her.

"You're definitely a farm girl! Good thing I didn't come out of my breeches."

Her face got hotter.

Just then she stubbed her toe on something and stumbled.

"Hey! Should you be walking around just yet?" he called out to her and she heard him come splashing out of the stream after her.

But Rhi couldn't move. She could only stare at what was before her and tremble. Her body had suddenly gone ice cold.

There were five mounds of newly turned earth before her...five graves.

Rhi suddenly realized why Shayne was bathing in the stream--to wash off all the grave dirt.

She heard him come up behind her and stop.

"I had to do something with the bodies, not just leave them here for the crows to pick at."

"Bodies," repeated Rhi. "They're bodies now. Just bodies."

The tone of her voice frightened Shayne. He took hold of her arms.

"Come, lass. You've no need to tarry here. Let's get you back to the fire and get some warm food into you."

He helped her back to her feet. Numbly she allowed him to guide her back to camp. He sat her down on a stump nearest the fire and wrapped her cloak around her because she had gone white with shock.

"Rhi? Say something, lass."

She finally spoke through trembling lips.

"I've never killed anyone before," she said in a whisper. "Chickens, ducks, rabbits to eat when we were hungry. But never another person."

Shayne busied himself spooning thick stew into a bowl for her.

"You had to, lass. He was going to rape and kill you. You had to do it," he reasoned.

"And you. You killed four men in the blink of an eye. Ended four lives as if it was nothing."

"It wasn't nothing!" Shayne almost snapped at her. "I was defending you. They would have killed you."

Then he grew quiet and thoughtful.

"But still. It's never 'nothing' when you kill a person. Whether they deserve it or not. It's never nothing."

Rhi's haunted eyes searched his face. Her voice was soft and distant.

"Yes, I know. I'm not questioning it had to be done."

She turned to him.

"Were those the first men you've ever killed? Or have there been more?"

This question brought him up cold.

"No. There have been other incidents like this. I have killed before."

They held each other's eyes.

"Was it always…justified?" she asked.

His eyes dropped in shame.

"So I have told myself."

He gave her a grim look. She was treading into areas of his life he did not want to talk about. He was still not sure he wanted to open the gates and let her in.

Rhi stared back into the flames of the fire.

"How do you get used to it, deal with it? The fact you robbed another human being of its life-force? How do you make peace with it?"

Shayne waited until her eyes met his.

"You don't. Not ever. You just try not to think about it."

He stirred his bowl of stew as if he had suddenly lost his appetite.

Rhi looked in the direction of the graves.

"Will they be angry ghosts? Because of how they died?" she asked.

"No," he replied in a firm voice.

She looked back at him confused.

The expression on his face was one of grim confidence.

"I will do a ritual tonight. My people have this thing we do for the spirits of dead adversaries. It takes their anger away and makes them rest peaceful."

She cocked her head at him like a curious dog.

"Do you always do this ritual?"

He sniffed.

"Well yeah! Bad things happen if I don't!"

Rhi looked at the stew in her bowl and stirred it. She took her first bite. "Someday you must tell me about your kinfolk."

Shayne smiled and the gloomy atmosphere lifted a bit. "Oh, I plan on it." He replied.

She did not look at him again. "You will disappear again soon," she said.

"What?"

"You can disappear. I've seen it. You will do so again. When will you disappear this time?"

He was silent for a long time.

"Not until you're healed enough to travel. I promise," he assured.

She sniffed.

"It is dangerous to make promises. They get you into trouble," she said in a voice devoid of all emotion.

"I'm well aware of the trouble promises can cause. I will not leave you unless you are safe. Then I'll open the cage door and set you free."

She nodded and said nothing.

NO CDAN'S LAND

Four days later he did leave her. Rhi rolled out of her bedroll to find the camp eerily quiet. He had taken the dead robber's horses and left. There was a pack of food left on a large flat rock.

Beside the pack, underneath a smaller stone was a note. As she unfolded it, a silver chain spilled out. She picked it up and inspected it closely. It was a thickly braided chain of a style she had never seen before. But she knew no horse trader could afford a chain of such expense. A rich merchant perhaps or an aristocrat would have the means to purchase such a costly item but not a mere seller of horses.

She knew immediately what the chain was for. All this time she had worn the medallion on a simple leather strap, one she had replaced many times over the years. She removed the medallion and took it off the leather and replaced it with the silver chain. The silver felt cool and light against her skin in spite of its thickness.

She turned her attention to the note. It was very short and to the point.

"I am sorry to leave you in such a secretive way as this, like a thief in the night. But the road calls me and I am compelled to follow. I take the memory of you with me. I beg you to be more careful in your travels. The world is a wide and dangerous place at times. You know this better now. But should you ever be in a dark place

again, you have only to call my name and I will appear. Please be careful and look after yourself and Falcon well. We will meet again. When I cannot say. But I am certain of it. I eagerly look forward to that day.

Farewell."

He had signed his name with the drawing of a feather.

She crumpled the letter. She was silent and still for a long while. She looked down the trail of hoof prints which led away from her camp. Her emotions were all jumbled. She felt angry and sad all at once and her chest felt tight.

She turned about and saw Falcon was watching her quietly as if he knew what she was thinking. He looked in the direction of the nearby road and then back to her. He too wanted to be back on the road.

She sighed and set her jaw resolutely.

"Come on, Falcon," she said. "Time to travel again."

They traveled for four days before they ran into another living soul.

They came to an intersection of the roads. The signpost was old and worn and Rhi could barely read the letters. The one sign pointed back and gave the name of the town she had left the robbers in. The other arm of the sign couldn't be read because the letters were so worn.

But a tinker happened to be coming the other way in his cart. He was an old man with a long beard and was followed by a scruffy dog. Rhi waved for him to stop. The pots and pans clanged as the tinker halted his rig next to her and his dog barked at them.

"What kingdom is that way?" she asked. "I can't read the sign."

The old tinker turned to look the way she pointed and squinted back at her.

"You can't read the sign 'cause there ain't no realm. Not anymore."

Rhi frowned.

"What happened? Do you know?"

The tinker laughed.

"Sure'n everybody local here knows what happened to it. But you're not local, I take it."

Rhi shrugged and her expression prodded him to continue.

"Time was there used to the great kingdom of Guthra. But not anymore. No one lives there now."

"But why? It looks like a beautiful country from here," she said.

"Oh it was and still is. Beautiful and blasted. Rich and cursed at all once. A dragon lord rules that land now. No one lives there but the dead. And if you enter, your family and friends will never see you again. The dragon does not like trespassers on his land. If you're smart, you'll turn around and go back. Then you'll live long enough to have grandchildren like me."

Rhi thought for a moment rolling her eyes.

"Go back? To the land of lecherous men? Never! If you give me a choice between one dragon and a town full of rude men, I'll take the dragon any day!"

The tinker shrugged.

"It's your funeral. I wouldn't set my pinky toe on the dragon's land if you ask me."

He snapped the reins on his mule's back and drove on.

"When the dragon comes to devour you, don't say I didn't warn you!"

The cart clattered on and the dog barked at her as they drove away.

Rhi took a deep breath and urged Falcon onward into the dragon's kingdom.

They rode at a steady pace that day and saw no other person. In fact they saw not another living thing all day, not a bird or a rabbit or even a butterfly. The land was eerily quiet except for the sound of the wind.

The countryside was beautiful; rugged and green with sweeping hills and mountains dotted with little hamlets and woodlands and gurgling streams and rivers. But every house she came to was abandoned...only the weeds and vines grew there.

As the sun dipped lower, she searched for a place to make camp.

She finally found a little clearing next to a burbling brook, wreathed by jagged rocks jutting out of the soil. She made a small fire and began to cook some food. She shook out her bedroll and prepared to spend the night there. The night was very cold and she wrapped herself tight in her cloak.

Falcon was grazing at the stream-bed when he suddenly whipped his head up and snorted.

Rhi jumped to attention and snapped her short sword out of its sheath.

A hooded figure stood just outside of the fire's light next to the jagged rocks. He seemed to have just melted out of the cold mist.

He stepped into the dancing fire's light and stopped. He removed his hood. He was a tall and incredibly handsome man. His hair was jet black and he was dressed in very fine clothes so Rhi assumed he was some sort of duke or somebody of great importance or rank. He wore an expensive and highly decorated sword on his hip.

His eyes were strange. They flashed in the dim dancing light so Rhi could not tell what color they actually were.

His expression was not a friendly one.

"What are you doing here?" he demanded curtly.

"Uh, making camp and cooking dinner."

He scowled at her.

"Do not be flippant with me! You are trespassing here. You must leave now!"

Rhi tried to calm him down and reason with him.

"Easy now. I'm sorry if I insulted you. I'm just passing through. I'll be gone soon enough."

"It's dangerous here. You need to leave, leave *NOW*!"

Rhi sighed.

"Look, I'm tired. I've ridden all day long and I'm hungry. I just need some food and some rest and I will gladly be on my way out of here."

The man put his hood back up and stepping backwards, once again melted into the shadows.

"You'll be dead!"

***

She awoke the next morning convinced it was all a bad dream caused by the old tinker's words and an active imagination while she slept. She rolled out of her bedroll, put the kettle on for tea and made breakfast. While it cooked she brushed and braided her long locks. After breakfast she doused the fire and saddled up Falcon.

The country steadily grew more lush and beautiful as they traveled. And the hamlets and scattered farms were still empty and abandoned.

She was going to stop for lunch in the center of a small village. But as she rode into the town square, she saw a sight which left her heart cold.

In front of Falcon's hooves were the sun-bleached bones of a small family. Their clothes were still hanging on their bones in weathered tatters. The woman's hair still clung in blonde patches to her skull and she hugged the bones of a small baby to her dead chest. The father was slightly ahead of them, lying face down his arms outstretched. They seem to have died as they were fleeing from some horrible enemy.

Rhi decided to press on and have her lunch elsewhere.

She stopped two hours later in a small field of abandoned wheat. A harsh crag of rock reared its rocky head above them not very far away and its peak looked like the rough hewn sculpture of a dragon.

She gazed at it for a long moment and shook her head. She thought this must be where people got the idea this vale was haunted by a dragon, from a great peak of rock, carved by nature, which looked like a dragon's head.

She shook her head and turned back to her meal. When she finished, she glanced back to the rocky peak and froze. Slowly she stood up, gazing intently at the rock face.

The dragon's head shape was gone. Now it was just a smooth outcrop of granite softened by the harsh winds.

Her skin prickled and she shivered although the day was warm.

She quickly packed up her belongings and rode away from the rocky crag.

She made her way at a much more brisk pace. Her eyes were constantly searching her surroundings for anything that wasn't quite right. Beautiful as this vale was, it was beginning to feel creepy to her.

She came across a small cottage with an attached stable right before sunset. She searched the grounds thoroughly but found no sign of another person, living or dead, not even graves for those who might have lived there. The roof was halfway caved in from neglect but there was enough dry area underneath the part which was still good for her and Falcon to rest comfortably for one night. There were storm clouds rolling in and Rhi could smell the rain that would soon arrive. She settled Falcon into the stable and began to collect deadfall for a fire. If it did rain hard she would need a fire.

Just as the last light was fading from the night, Rhi straightened. She tried to bend the kinks out of her back and that was when she saw it.

Far off in the distance, against the dark clouds of the sky, a great, black shape soared. Its bat-like wings were enormous and they were attached to a snake-like body.

Rhi snatched up her firewood and bolted for the hidden recesses of the cottage.

The old tales were true. There was a dragon in the vale!

She huddled in the farthest, driest corner of the cottage and tried to be very still. She thought long and hard about the wisdom of lighting a fire this night. Rain or no rain, it was going to be a very chilly, raw evening. She wondered if dragons could fly in the rain.

She finally decided to chance it. That and her fingers and toes were already nearly frozen. Shivering half from cold, half from apprehension, she built a small fire in the fireplace.

She thought about the warning the tinker had given her. She thought about the skeletons of the poor family she had encountered earlier that day. She thought about the dragon stone she had seen and the dragon in the sky just now. Had she really seen it or were her eyes playing tricks with her? And she wondered about the disturbing dream she had had the night before. Was it really a dream?

Wrapped up in her woolen cloak, poking the fire to keep it alive enough to heat her, she finally nodded off.

Her senses awakened her later that night. It was raining; a nice, soft gentle rain with lightning and thunder in the distance.

She shook herself, added another log to the fire and stabbed at it with a stick to wake it up enough to put out more heat.

Then the lightning flashed and she knew she was no longer alone in the cottage. She pinched herself to make sure she was awake this time. Slowly she turned around.

The man from the night before stood in the doorway to the cottage. He stepped inside and removed his rain soaked hood. He looked around at her meager surroundings.

"Are you moving in now?" he asked with some heat.

She was almost relieved to see a person and not a dragon standing there. She cleared her throat.

"Excuse me, but your kingdom is a large one. It will take me more than one day to cross it. But I assure you I am on my way out of it."

He frowned at her.

"Are all people from your land as thick as you? You are trespassing! You need to leave now. Period."

She took a deep breath and once again tried to reason with him.

"I am sorry for the intrusion, really I am," she said.

Her apology seemed to startle him.

"But the weather outside is awful. Please come sit with me and I will share what food I have. It won't be fancy but it will be hot. Please, sir."

He didn't seem to know how to respond to her apology or invitation.

"It's dangerous here. You need to leave before something bad happens to you."

"I will leave," she assured him. "Tomorrow morning when the rain has stopped. Now come and eat with me."

He shook his head and stepped back away from her.

"You'll be dead," he repeated.

There was another flash of lightning and he was gone.

***

She spent a very cold and fitful night in the cottage, tormented by strange dreams and a fire which didn't seem to want to catch. She finally gave up on it.

In the morning she ate a cold breakfast and packed her supplies as quickly as possible. Luckily the rain had stopped just before dawn. She saddled and bridled Falcon and they were on their way again.

Rhi half loved this kingdom and half wanted to never see it again. So she pushed Falcon on with as much speed as she dared.

Their way took them steadily downward, off the mountain slopes and into the wide valley beyond. Here there were more farmlands and even more cottages. But like all the others, there was still no sign of any people.

The nice thing about being in the valley was that the weather improved. It got much warmer to the point that Rhi actually had to stop and pack away her cloak and change into her lightest summer attire. She had braided her hair in a long, reddish brown plait down her back to keep her cooler. She ate a quick meal and was on her way again, eager to put as many miles between her nighttime stops.

Around mid-afternoon she came to a surprising sight. Falcon climbed the crest of a small hill and she halted him. Off in the distance, on a small rise of ground, surrounded by a large city was a white castle.

Its sides glistened like alabaster as if the whitewash was fresh and had yet to dry and it glistened, shining wetly in the sun. No vines crawled on its sides, its roofs were not caved in. Of all the habitations which surrounded it, it seemed to be the only thing which was well tended and looked after.

And soaring in the sky above it, like some gigantic bird of prey, floated an immense red, golden dragon. It made two passes around the castle and then landed lightly on the highest parapet. It swung its great head in her direction. It was so far away Rhi could not see its great eyes glittering at her. But she knew it could see her.

It gaped its great mouth to the sky and cried out in a voice she had never heard before. She shuddered and her heart grew cold with fear.

Falcon startled underneath her and when the dragon cried out he reared. Rhi stuck to him like glue. She felt him trembling in fear beneath her. When his forelegs touched the earth, he danced, wanting to run. Rhi released her tight hold on the reins and let him.

Dragons eat horses, don't they? she thought to herself. If they did, then she was sure the rider would just be an added seasoning to the dish, just another hors d'oeuvres. She let Falcon run as hard and fast as he wanted and just concentrated on staying with him.

As his powerful legs churned beneath her, Rhi risked a look back at the dragon perched on the castle top.

It just sat there watching them. It did not take to the air and pursue them. It just watched. Rhi was certain it could see them. She could feel its fiery eyes boring into her back. But it made no move to give chase. It just sat there staring.

This only frightened her all the more.

She let Falcon run. He galloped hard and fast as if the hounds of hell itself were chasing them. Rhi's only move was to guide his terrified charge. If the dragon did chase them it would be harder to pursue them under cover. She guided him onto a woodland trail. Soon the trees hid them from all sight from above. Falcon ran until he was winded and sweat foamed around his tack. Rhi slowly took more and more control back in the reins and rated his speed. She finally had him slowed down to a less panicked gait but he was puffing and blowing from the exertion. She walked him several hours until he had caught his breath and his brain had returned to his head.

She kept him to woodland trails the rest of the day and rode him well after dusk. Exhaustion finally convinced them both to stop and rest. Here it was the third night and they were still in the dragon's kingdom. All Rhi wanted was to leave this land far behind, no matter how beautiful it was. The dragon could keep it.

Wearily she made camp next to a large river. She untacked Falcon and walked him into the center of the river to wash the dried sweat off. She swam a little herself because in spite of it being after dark, the weather was still very warm and the ice melted snow water from the mountains felt good.

She led him out of the river and hobbled him on a thickly grassed embankment where he could graze in peace. After sight of the dragon, she decided against a fire and a hot dinner. Besides it was too warm for a fire or even a blanket to sleep under. All she wanted was cold water and sleep.

And she wanted to be out of this land!

She shook out her wet hair and combed it with her fingers.

"You're still here."

The voice startled her and she spun about, her hands still tangled in her hair.

The man from the past two nights stood behind her, scowling at her in the light of the full moon.

"I have been very lenient with you because you're a beautiful young woman traveling alone in a strange land. But there are limits to my leniency."

Rhi sighed.

"Look! I'm trying to be as nice to you as I know how. I've told you I'm leaving and I am. Now if you have any suggestions as to how I can traverse this land quicker, I would be happy to hear them."

He took a step closer to her.

"People do not traverse my land. They die when they set foot on my land."

Rhi sighed in frustration and, untangling her fingers from her hair, she flung the locks behind her and spread her arms wide.

"Then please tell me how I can get out of here safely and quickly."

He was silent.

Rhi looked at him and found he had suddenly gone stiff as a statue. His eyes were locked on her and he seemed to be shocked.

He slowly pointed at her.

"Where did you get that medallion?"

She realized her new summer garb left her throat rather open to view. Her fingers touched the braided, silver chain.

"It was…a gift," she said quietly.

His eyes turned back to her face. He seemed less angry and more curious.

"A gift?" he repeated. "From whom?"

She swallowed carefully. Why did she suddenly not want to tell him?

"I command you to tell me who gave you that silver talisman!"

Oh, this is how it's going to be eh? she thought. He seemed awfully comfortable with barking orders and getting what he wanted. He must be royalty.

"No one important. Just a simple horse trader."

The man facing her smiled and squinted one eye. Then he chuckled.

"Just a simple horse trader, eh?" he said. "Who are you? What is your name?"

She shrugged.

"Rhiannon."

"Rhiannon," he repeated. His smile got bigger. "My dear, we must talk. And I will not take no for an answer. "

He suddenly began to chant in words she did not understand. Before she could do anything, she felt her vision grow dark and her limbs grow weak.

Then she fainted dead away.

the Gilded Cage

She awoke to what she thought was a tapestry hung above her head. When she turned her head to either side she saw instead she was in a spacious room lying on a canopy bed.

She sat up and took greater interest in her surroundings.

The room dripped luxury and wealth. It seemed to be decorated for a princess. There was gold trim and lacing around the corners of the room, a wide vanity with a mirror and an enormous wardrobe to one side. There was a fireplace on the other side and the foot of the bed faced a floor to ceiling window through which the morning sun was shining.

She had a stray thought. She ran to the windows, pushed them open and stepped onto the narrow balcony beyond.

It was all as she had suspected. She was in the dragon's castle!

As if she needed more proof of the fact, she felt the wind whoosh over her head. Rhi looked up and stared into the white underbelly of the dragon as it flew overhead her balcony. It banked in its flight, turned itself about and just hovered in midair. Its faceted eyes glittered like jewels and it lolled its tongue out as it laughed at her.

With a gasp of fright, she fled back indoors and slammed the windows closed. She ran to the farthest corner of the room and huddled against the floor shaking in terror.

How did she get here?

The dragon outside her window only laughed harder making the room shudder. She heard the great wings flap as it flew away.

She buried her head in her arms and whimpered. She just huddled there for a long time. She had no idea how long she sat, trying to convince herself it was all a bad dream. But she finally came back to her senses when she heard a gentle rap on the door.

It opened and a man dressed like a servant stepped in and proceeded to wait.

Slowly, cautiously, Rhi stood up and approached him.

"Hello?" she said.

The man turned to face her. He seemed utterly human and yet his eyes were blank and devoid of all emotion. Rhi passed a hand in front of his face. He did not react at all. His eyes never followed her hand, he did not smile or acknowledge the motion. He seemed to be both deaf and mute.

The strange man reached to her but stopped just short of touching her. He then gestured with the other hand she was to come with him. All the time he did not speak nor did his eyes focus on anything.

Mutely she obeyed.

He led her to an adjoining room. More people dressed like castle staff were gathered there. They all seemed to have the same affliction as this one man. They never spoke, or showed any emotion or looked at anything. They were just bustling about doing their jobs like automatons.

This room was obviously a room for bathing. There was a huge deep fireplace with a roaring fire set up and iron spigots with kettles of water hung to heat suspended. The women servants were filling a large bathtub with steaming hot water.

A large woman with vacant eyes came up to her and motioned she was to strip and bathe. Rhi hesitated but then did as she was bid. As Rhi slid into the hot water another servant girl came approached and offered a tray with a pat of lard soap and fragrantly scented oils. The servant girl looked past Rhi to the blank wall. Rhi bathed and scrubbed herself and soaped her long hair. It did feel good to actually have a hot bath and scrub off all the trail grime. When she stepped out of the bath, two more blank faced women descended on her with towels to dry her with and a comb for her hair. She waved them off and relieved them of the towels and comb. She saw no need for someone else to dry her!

She was accompanied back to her room where a modest woman's dress had been set out for her. She would have preferred a tunic and breeches but she had no idea what they had done with her packs.

A sumptuous lunch was provided by another soulless servant carrying a silver tray. She spent the rest of a very boring day looking out the window and pacing her room. She wanted to find Falcon and leave but the man servant refused to let her do so.

About an hour before dusk, she saw the dragon fly back to the castle and take roost on the highest parapet above her window.

A servant appeared to light her room for the evening. Another appeared and went to the wardrobe. He chose an evening gown of silver and gold and laid it on the great canopy bed. He pointed to the dress and then to her.

Apparently she was expected to don the dress.

She grumbled but did as he bid.

Another servant, a woman this time, entered her room and pointed to the vanity with the mirror. Growling slightly in displeasure, Rhi sat down and allowed her hair to be coiffed by this servant who acted blind. Her hair was brushed and braided, piled and pinned and bejeweled until the vacant faced, blind woman seemed to think her work was done and stepped back.

Rhi looked at her reflection in the mirror. A truly stunning woman gazed back at her. She saw her reflection and frowned. Yes, beautiful she may be but it didn't feel right to her. She wanted her hair back in a simple braid down her back. She wanted a white tunic and brown breeches and riding boots. That was how Rhi liked to dress. Not like this!

Certainly not for....just what was she getting all dressed up for? She looked to the servants and knew they wouldn't tell her anything.

Another man servant appeared and gestured that she was to come with him. She gathered up her noisy gown and followed.

The servant led her down a long hallway, down a flight of steps, through a small atrium down another flight of steps into a large dining hall with a long table set for two.

Her dinner host was already there.

The man that had appeared to her every night since she had entered the forbidden kingdom stood next to his throne like chair at the head of the table. He was dressed all in gold and saffron and there was a modest circlet of gold set upon his head.

He smiled when he saw her.

"Greetings, my lady. I am King Nazar of the province of Guthra. And I am honored you would join me for dinner."

Rhi raised her chin slightly. *So that was it, eh?* she thought to herself. *He wasn't a duke or a mere aristocrat. He was the bloody king!* She remembered stories from her family and the people she grew up with about kings and how they treated people of her station. Her kin were cannon fodder to them. She quickly reassessed how she was going to handle the situation. She wanted to be flippant and curt to him but it just might get her killed. Best to play the part to the hilt and secretly find out what his plans were for her. Any hastiness might cost her dearly.

She took a deep breath. Problem was putting on such an act would be a lot more difficult for her than what she really wanted to do. If she slipped up by saying or doing the wrong thing... She sucked her teeth. Being a mere farm girl was so much easier and less complicated.

"Much better," King Nazar was saying to her. "The dress flatters you nicely, my dear."

"I'm glad you like it," she replied because it was the expected response. Then she stumbled into silence. Now what was she supposed to do?

He pulled out the chair for her and motioned for her to be seated. His manners were impeccable. She had no idea how to act or behave.

Mutely, she seated herself.

He returned to his own throne at the head of the table and seated himself.

She waited until he picked up his knife and fork before she began to eat. When she did eat, she just nibbled although the spread was lavish. Rhi's thoughts were spinning. She had no idea as to the next thing she should do or was supposed to or expected to do. So she simply let him to go first. She allowed him to lead the conversation and interjected only when he asked a question of her directly.

She found the whole experience maddening! She wanted to jump to her feet, throw the wine glass in his face and demand he return her things and Falcon to her and let her leave. But she couldn't do that. She had to be civil. She had to be proper. She had to be polite. She hated the whole experience and fumed inwardly.

The dinner progressed quite peacefully until the end. Then Rhi couldn't stand it. She had to ask just one, tiny, question.

"Sire, am I your prisoner here?"

King Nazar looked at her, really looked this time. It was as if he suspected that this was all some act of protocol.

Then the face of royalty returned.

"My dear, you misunderstand my intentions. It is I who is a prisoner to you and your charms."

Oh, how she wanted to slap him right then and there! She clenched her fists but restrained herself from doing any more.

"You may only see me at night. I am busy during the day. But during the day you are free to roam anywhere your heart desires within these castle walls."

Her heart skipped a beat. She felt the doors of her gilded cage closing all about her.

"Am I permitted to ride my horse?" she asked as she rose to leave.

He looked at her narrowly.

"Rhiannon, you no longer have any need of a horse. You are not permitted to leave the castle at any time day or night. If you do, my servants have orders to kill you. Is that understood?"

Rhi's heart pounded in her ears. All she could do was nod in acquiescence.

She felt the doors of her prison clang shut and lock.

***

He had permitted her to explore the castle. So the next day she did go exploring. She noticed wherever she went, there were the same people following her. They may have been dressed like kitchen staff, servants, maids or soldiers but they were all the same. They all had human bodies with blank, staring eyes, soulless and lifeless except for the job they were supposed to do. Whenever she tried to get free and alone she would see one step around the corner and just stand there, observing, watching. She felt like she was being followed by ghosts.

She first went to see if she could find a stable. Most castles had a courtyard and a barn. Maybe he had hidden Falcon there.

She found the courtyard easily enough and yes, it had a stable. But there were no horses or any other livestock for that matter that she could see. The hay was musty, the grain moldy and any piles of manure were white and so dried out that they crumbled to dust when kicked.

There was no sign of Falcon. She even whistled for him but received no answering whinny.

What had Nazar done to him? Did he hide him or just feed him to the dragon? The not knowing was the worst part.

She sighed and made her way back up inside the castle. She noticed underneath a lofty archway leading away from the courtyard there was a large pile of stone rubble. She looked up to the keystone of the archway. There was a bright, shiny new shield embossed with the emblem of the castle, a great, red golden dragon. She surmised the pile of stone rubble must be the remains of the last family's symbol who lived in the castle before the dragon took up residence. She knelt down and carefully arranged the pieces of the old plaque back together again like the pieces of a puzzle. When all the broken pieces were assembled together, the picture on the plaque was of a small falcon.

Rhi began to search throughout the castle for any high vaulted doorway which had the dragon plaque on it. She always found a smashed plaque somewhere around the base and when reassembled it always had the picture of a falcon.

All were like this but one. The last one she assembled held the picture of a feather in silver paint. Rhi gasped and stood up. She looked at the silver medallion she wore around her neck.

The feathers were identical.

She stepped into the room it once had guarded. It was a child's play room. Toys were scattered about gathering dust. Along the wall was a small collection of toy horses of all shapes and sizes and colors. There was a large rocking horse there covered in gray. Rhi stepped over to it and quietly, sadly brushed the gray powder off its forehead. She then gasped again and clapped both hands over her mouth in surprise.

The rocking horse was painted to resemble a coppery, red chestnut with a white star on its forehead like wings.

"Falcon!" Rhi whispered. She fled back to her room and stayed there the rest of the day.

That night the same ritual happened. The same servants came into her room and lit the candles and lanterns. Another man servant went to the great wardrobe and picked out another dress, this time one of deep midnight blue trimmed in silver and gestured for her to put it on. The same woman servant styled her hair. And the same butler led her down to dinner with the king, her captor.

She had a similar sumptuous feast with him, exchanged the same useless but appropriate banter.

And again at the end of the feast she dared to ask a question.

"For how long am I to be your guest, my lord?" she asked quietly.

He looked at her as if it was a strange inquiry. "Forever, of course," was his reply. "Oh my dear, do not look so hopeless! I can provide you with such pleasures that a person of your station could only dream of. You have only to ask and I will furnish you with it. You want gold and jewels I can give you that. Fine dresses and any pretty thing your heart could possibly desire. Your stay here could be as pleasant as you could possibly imagine. Or it could be otherwise."

He let the subtle threat hang in the air between them.

She did not dare to ask for details. She just trembled, nodded and retired quietly to her room.

But it seemed to her that the walls of her gilded cage were pressing in on her.

***

She investigated the castle more the next day, choosing to climb to the highest parapets long after the dragon had left for the day. She found the perch the dragon used by the claw marks gouging great trenches into the top level.

But she soon bored of wandering around and returned to her room to strategize how she would handle this night's conversation. She decided she wanted more information out of him. But she would have to be very sweet to the king and make him think he had a chance with her.

That night a green and silver gown was set out for her to wear. Her hair was plaited and piled and suitably pinned with gems and silver. And she was led down to the expected dinner with her captor lord.

58

She, as planned, was very sweet to him. She laughed at all his jokes even if she did not find them amusing at all. She even allowed him to hold her hand and kiss it.

He seemed to be playing right into her plans, staring romantically into her eyes and leaning towards her, his meal forgotten.

"Oh my lord," she said smiling sweetly up at him. "Why did you threaten me so our first night? Was it really necessary? You couldn't possibly kill me now could you?"

And she leaned her soft cheek against his hand.

His hand was suddenly pulled away and his eyes grew dark and hard. He gestured to his man servant as he pushed himself back in his throne. Then he whispered in the servant's ear and waved him away.

Looking back to her he sniffed and smiled.

"Let me show you what I can do," he said and his expression was no longer romantic.

Five young women were led into the room. They were all beautiful and all as blank face and soulless eyes as the other servants.

"What is this?" Rhi asked warily.

"These are some of my most precious possessions." Nazar told her. "I found five pretty birds. They were each so lovely that I could not let them fly free. Something bad might happen to them. So I caught them and put them here in my golden cage where they would be safe from all harm the cruel world might do to them. I gave them every little thing a pretty bird might want. I even asked each one of them to marry me. And still they were not happy."

His eyes shifted to meet Rhi's gaze.

"So I separated them from their souls. Now they do whatever I tell them to do, whenever I tell them to do it. It doesn't matter now if they are happy or not. They're just birds, pretty to look at and play with but of no good use for anything really important other than my amusement."

His gaze held her eyes. They were cold and hard. "Now I have found a sixth pretty bird to add to my collection."

Rhi felt her chest get tight and it was getting very hard for her to breathe. "Please excuse me, sire. I believe I need some fresh air."

He nodded and waved her away. "Of course you do. I've given you a lot to think about. Until tomorrow night, my lady."

She found she had a hard time walking calmly away from the table and out of his presence. She either wanted to faint or run. She was trembling so badly her knees were knocking. She refused to faint.

So she ran. She ran through the castle. She had no idea where she was going just that she needed someplace which didn't have a roof over her head. She needed to feel the free wind on her face and in her hair. She needed to ride Falcon fast and far away from this place.

But Falcon was gone so she ran to the courtyard.

By the time she got there, her lungs burned and her legs ached. It had been a long time since she had used her own legs to run anywhere. She collapsed in a heap of green silk and silver trim. She gasped for breath. The free wind buffeted her face and cooled her heated skin. She turned her face up to the night sky and sobbed. She was trapped again and it was all her fault. This would have never happened if she had not taken the left fork in the road.

Both her hands found the silver medallion she wore about her neck.

"Shayne!" she sobbed. "Please help me. I'm in a cage again. Please help."

There was a flash of light the minute the words left her lips.

And he was there just as he had promised, standing before her as she knelt in silk and diamonds at his feet.

"Rhiannon?" he said in confusion.

And bending down, he stroked her expertly styled, bejeweled hair. "What's happened to you?"

She realized Shayne barely recognized her dressed as she was.

Then he looked about him at his surroundings. "You're...here?" he said slowly and his voice had a strange ring that she had never heard before. "How? Why are you here?"

"The dragon lord has caught me and won't let me leave," she said.

He spun about at her words. "Dragon lord? Did you tell him your name?"

Rhi climbed to her feet. "Well, yes. He asked."

Shayne uttered a word in another language she didn't understand. He ran his fingers through his hair and danced in a circle in frustration.

"*Never* tell him your name! Do you hear me? Never! That's how he catches you!"

Rhi had never seen him so upset.

Then a voice shouted from behind them. It shouted one word, a word Rhi didn't recognize.

"Oh no!' Shayne said and his face blanched white.

"What is it?"

Soldiers began to materialize out of the shadowed recesses of the courtyard, lots and lots of soldiers.

"I can't help you, Rhi. He has my secret name. My magic is useless here."

"What? How is that possible?" Rhi cried out as she saw soldiers headed for her now.

She turned back to see that four soldiers had grabbed Shayne, taken his sword and were dragging him away. He struggled and thrashed but he could not fight them off.

"You need to save *me* this time!" he called after her.

She felt the dead hands of two soldiers take hold of her arms. "Shayne!" she screamed.

"Save me, Rhiannon! You're the only one who can!"

And with that the darkness swallowed him up.

NOBLE LIES

Rhi was bodily dragged back into the castle. The servants pulled her, kicking and struggling, up the stairs.

At the top of the stairs stood King Nazar. She stopped fighting. For a long moment they just regarded each other. The king had a strange smirk on his face, almost as if he had expected this to happen.

Rhi felt her heart hammer in her chest. She half expected him to unsheathe his sword and cut off her head right then and there. But he didn't.

Finally he waved the servants on and turned away.

"Until tomorrow night, my lady," was all he said to her.

She was taken back to her room and shoved unceremoniously inside. The door was slammed and she heard the key turn in the lock.

She went to the bed and buried her face in her hands.

She had trapped them both. If she hadn't chosen this path she would never be here, held as a hostage, like a bird in a beautifully gilded cage. And through calling out for help she had unwittingly trapped Shayne too, the only man who could possibly save her.

What a mess she had made of things! Now what was going to happen?

She might as well just give in and do whatever the dragon lord asked of her. She burst into tears and cried herself to sleep. She awoke the next morning to a cloudy day and a new frame of mind.

Just as every morning before, the dragon swooped low over her window and left on its daily flight around the kingdom.

The door opened and a servant came in with a silver tray bearing her breakfast. He placed it on the small dining table in her room and stood waiting.

Rhi looked him up and down thinking hard.

"You, man!" she said in a commanding voice.

The servant turned to face her. His eyes were still blank.

"Am I now allowed to leave my room?" she asked.

The servant turned to the side and held his arm out to the door.

So they could respond if ordered correctly, she thought.

"Am I allowed to wander wherever I wish within this castle?"

The servant blinked and nodded once.

"Am I allowed to travel outside the castle?"

The servant blinked twice and shook his head no.

"Hmmm," muttered Rhi thinking. "Bring me a maid servant, please."

The servant nodded and left.

Rhi stood up and went to the dining table. She caught a glimpse of herself in the vanity mirror as she strode past. She looked a sight! Half of her was all dolled up for a party, the other half all wrinkled up with fly away hair like she had just been rolled down a street.

Her hands went to her hair and she began to undo the hairstyle from the night before and pick out all the gems.

The servant girl stepped into her room.

"Ah good. There you are," she said. "Look, see here. I want my old clothes back. Them or a close enough replacement. I want a tunic, breeches and riding boots. Go get these for me now. I order you to obey me."

The woman blinked twice, nodded and left.

Rhi sat down to eat, a plan taking shape in her head. She had barely finished when the servant girl returned with some items she arranged on the bed for her inspection.

They were not her clothes. But they were the attire of a man.

There was a white tunic and a leather vest, brown breeches and tall black riding boots. Rhi nodded. They would do if they fit.

She stood up and busied herself with getting out of this grand get up which she had been forced to wear. She kicked the rich dress to the side. She never wanted to see or wear it again. She hurriedly donned the clothes the maid had provided her. Everything fit perfectly.

She sighed in relief and hugged herself. It felt so good to be wearing real clothes again!

She removed all the pins and gems from her tresses and brushed out and braided her hair in one long plait. She then inspected her reflection in the mirror and nodded. This was so much better! She looked like a real human being again, much more like the old Rhi.

She hailed one of the man servants.

"Do you have a dungeon in this castle?" she asked.

The servant nodded wordlessly.

"Good. Take me there," she commanded.

The servant blinked twice, then turned about and led her out of the room. She followed him wordlessly. He led her down a maze of stairs into areas of the castle she hadn't explored yet. Their progress was steadily downward. She knew they were underground when the windows suddenly disappeared.

They reached a dark spiral staircase. Here the servant stopped and lit a torch. He then handed it to her and motioned she was to go on alone. She took the torch from him and taking a deep breath, plunged down the stairs.

It was a good thing she took the breath. It was the last fresh air there was. The stench of dank, moldy walls and rotting other things she did not want to think about wafted up to her from the dark recesses before her.

She reached the bottom and peered about. The torchlight didn't go very far. She had no idea how big the room was. She picked a direction and headed that way. A stone wall soon reared up before her eyes and to it was chained a bearded skeleton. She squeaked in surprise, almost dropping the torch. She clapped a hand over her mouth to keep from screaming and backed away.

There was a scrape of something moving in the darkness. She spun about at the sound but couldn't see what made it.

"Rhi? Is that you or am I dreaming?"

"Shayne?" she called out.

"Over here! Behind you," the raspy voice directed.

She turned about and walked in the dark direction. Floor to ceiling iron bars suddenly loomed out of the darkness. A white hand reached out of the murky depths towards her. It was attached to something light colored crouched on the floor pressed up against them.

It was Shayne. He was beaten up and bruised but alive.

Rhi ran to him and fell to the floor to sit beside him.

"Just let me touch you to make sure you're real. I've had so many horrible dreams of late."

She grabbed the bars and pressed herself close to them. He touched her face with trembling hands.

"I knew you were in trouble," he whispered to her. "For days I've had dreams you were here. Terrible dreams. I was hoping I was wrong. Now I find they were true."

She sniffed. "I was trying to take care of this by myself. I was trying not to call for you."

He stroked her face through the bars. "You can't. Nazar is too powerful especially when he's in his own kingdom. And he never leaves."

"Then we're both trapped here."

She felt his forehead nod against hers. "I hate this place," he told her. "Not just the cell. I hate this whole castle. It reminds me of all the mistakes I have made that I can't ever take back or change. I never wanted to come back here. Too many bad memories, too many ghosts from the past."

Rhi shuddered at his words and tried not to think about how many ghosts were possibly haunting the dungeon.

"But your cell seems a lot nicer than mine," he tried to jest. His laughter fell into the silence and was swallowed up.

"What will he do to you?" she asked.

"Nothing. Just leave me here to die of thirst and hunger. He never takes care of his prisoners. He just starves them to death."

She groaned. "I'll bring you food every day until I figure something out," she promised.

He nodded, looking hopelessly at the floor.

"What will he do to me?" she asked.

Shayne sighed. "Don't! I don't want to think about that right now."

But she wouldn't be put off. "Shayne please! I need to know."

He sighed again and his hands clenched into fists on the bars. "Every night he will dress you up like a princess and have dinner with you. And every night at the end of dinner, he will propose marriage. He will do this every night for a month. The last night, if you persist in refusing him…he will remove your soul from your body. You will be dead but not dead. Like all the others up there. When he asks you to marry him, your time is short."

He swallowed with difficulty. "Normally he just runs off any stranger he meets or kills them. But you've done something to catch his fancy. He finds you interesting so he'll keep you around. He'll try to break you if you refuse to marry him."

She was silent for a long moment. "Then I guess I will have to marry him," she said blankly.

"*NO!*" Shayne said and grabbed her shoulders. "There's got to be some other way. Please just put him off until we figure something out. Please, Rhi!"

She hissed and pulled away from him. "Then what would you have me do? I cannot leave here. He has forbidden it. He says if I leave the castle I will die. I'm not sure whether he's telling the truth or just trying to frighten me."

"Both!" Shayne insisted. "Frightened people are more obedient. And if you leave this castle you *will* die. I've seen it happen before."

Shayne took hold of her hands. "Please give me a chance to figure this out. There may still be a way we can escape here. Every spell has its counter-spell."

Rhi sighed. "I never want to wear another one of those abominable dresses ever again!" she said squeezing her eyes shut against the thought. "Will he kill me if I show up for dinner like this?"

Shayne laughed and looked her up and down approvingly. "Well, I certainly prefer it!" he said and then he uttered a heavy sigh. "No, he will not kill you for wearing it. But he will not be pleased about it either. You will aggravate him and he has very little toleration for being aggravated. Just like a dragon. You do not poke a dragon if you mean to live long."

"Well I mean to live long and I mean to poke him! I've had it with being demur and polite!"

Shayne reached out and stroked her cheek. "I would never make you wear a dress if you didn't want to. I would just make you ride horses to the end of your days."

She smiled and leaned against the bars. "That doesn't sound so bad."

She wanted to stay there all day with him. She wanted to open the cell's great iron bars and set him free. She looked about, inspecting the bars more closely.

"Where is the lock for these bars? Where is the door?" she asked as she searched.

"It has none. It's magical. It stays open until it has an occupant and then the bars become a solid wall, no doors, no lock. His prisoners do not come and go. They just get thrown in and left."

She groaned. "What kind of man is this King Nazar? A tyrant?"

Shayne smiled. "Yes, that's all he's ever aspired to be. Bad to the core."

Rhi had no idea how she was going to save Shayne. She needed more information. However the collection of the information meant she had to brave Nazar again.

***

That night, once again the servant arrived in her room before the evening meal. A dress was laid out for her, this time one of gold and silver. A maid appeared to style her hair.

Rhi stepped away from them.

"No," she refused.

They gestured to the dress and vanity again.

"No," she insisted. "I go dressed like this or I don't go at all."

And before they had a chance to gesture more, she walked out of the room without them.

"Excuse me. I think I know the way," she told them.

She strode alone through the castle, down the stairs and into the dining hall unescorted. The king shot to his feet when he saw her.

"My lady, you are not properly attired for dinner!" he said.

He looked at her dressed in a tunic, breeches and riding boots with a disapproving eye.

"You look like a post man!" he said in disgust.

"Then you will have dinner with a post man," she stated firmly. "And I am not your lady…yet!"

She did not wait for him to assist her, she seated herself.

Slowly he sat down after her, scowling all the while.

"Why did you not wear the dress I assigned for you?" he growled.

She looked him fully in the face. "I did not like the dress," she replied.

"There were others," he muttered. "And the jewels?"

"I do not like the jewels," she replied. "Look King Nazar. Let's get one thing straight between us. You do not like to be told no. I accept that. I do not like to have every aspect of my life dictated and controlled. You need to know this before we go any further."

She took a deep cleansing and bracing breath before continuing. "Now if anything I have recently said has displeased you, you are free to lop off my head with that sword of yours."

She faced him squarely her jaw set, her eyes blue steel, almost daring him to do it.

He just glared back at her, too surprised to know how to respond. The air between them was electric.

"Fine!" he declared at last, slamming his palms onto the table top. "It seems I am having dinner with a lady postman!"

Inwardly she breathed an immense sigh of relief. She had survived the first hurdle. Now came all the others.

"Am I having dinner with the real Rhiannon, then?" he asked.

"Yes, you are."

"Then I will speak plainly," Nazar said.

"I wish you would!" she replied. "All this senseless polite banter and small talk is quite tiring to me."

He smiled back. "Quite."

She could see the wheels in his head turning, trying to best figure out how he could use this to his advantage.

"Tell me about this horse trader who gave you that medallion," he said.

Rhi swallowed her bite carefully. "There's not much to tell really. He's a horse trader. I bought my horse from him, the horse which has suddenly gone missing and no one seems to know what happened to him. He gave me this medallion. I guess he liked me some. That's it. End of story."

"Yes, of course," King Nazar replied smiling smugly as if he suspected more than she was telling. "A horse dealer who is in my dungeon right now. A horse dealer with a touch of magic to him. A horse dealer you begged to rescue you from me. A horse dealer whose name is Shayne."

She took another deep breath and struggled to control her emotions from showing on her face. She tried not to seem too upset by this.

She calmly shrugged and sipped from her wine glass. "If you know more about him I'd be glad to hear it. He's not much of a talker."

The king's smile only increased. "You really do know nothing about him do you?" he purred maliciously.

"Is there a story to him?" she asked innocently.

He chuckled. "Quite a story my dear. He killed my father. He's also my brother."

Her fork clattered to the plate, food suddenly forgotten.

It couldn't be possible.

Shayne was a kinslayer?

***

"Now I know why you never wanted to tell me about your past!" she fumed at him the next day.

Shayne's face wrinkled in confusion. "What has he told you?"

"He told me enough!" she spouted. "He told me you killed your own father!"

Shayne's face went dark and angry. "No," he whispered.

"Kinslayer!" she shouted at him. "You're a murdering kinslayer!"

"*NO!*" Shayne replied his voice raised in warning. "I *never* killed my father. I never would do such a thing."

"He also said you were brothers. Is it true? Shayne, are you a prince?"

Shayne clutched the bars of his cell tight until his knuckles turned white.

"I'm the second-born. I'm not important. Just an insurance policy to the throne. Yes, Nazar is my brother. But I never killed my father. *Never!* He's lying to you."

Rhi was so upset she was pacing back and forth. "How am I to believe that? Who is telling the truth?"

She grabbed the bars of his jail cell and spat at him. "You're both lying to me!"

Shayne raised his chin a bit. "So the lass doesn't like being lied to. Duly noted."

She sniffed in scorn and turned to leave. Shayne caught her arm and pulled her back. His grip was strong.

"Don't you dare leave here until I tell you this."

She tried unsuccessfully, to jerk her arm back.

"What? More lies?"

He shook her arm. "No. More truths."

She hesitated. He had her interest.

He sighed and released her. His hands pleaded for patience. "If you want to really know who to believe, ask him about his pet dragon."

Her eyes searched his face. "What's the dragon got to do with this?"

"Everything! Haven't you ever wondered why you only see the dragon during the day and him at night? Because he *IS* the dragon! Go to the uppermost parapet where you see the claw marks on the stone at dawn. You will see him turn into a dragon. Then come back and tell me I have no reason to keep secrets from anyone!"

Rhi stared at him for a long moment.

She then turned and fled from his presence. This was madness! She had no idea who or what to believe anymore.

***

She stayed in her room all day thinking. Her world had gotten very complicated all of a sudden. How did this happen?

What Shayne had said was ludicrous. No one could turn into a dragon! But not too long ago she had believed dragons weren't real, just fictitious monsters in fairy tales told to children to keep them good. Now she was learning the fairy tales were real and the world could be a very horrible place sometimes filled with very bad people and situations that weren't all black and white. There were too many shades of gray.

She heaved a heavy sigh and looked through the great window at the road leading away from the castle, a road which was forbidden to her. How was she going to get out of this mess?

She toyed with the silver medallion around her neck and wished for the thousandth time in the last few days she was someplace else.

Then the dragon appeared in the sky in the distance. First it was a tiny, spindly speck but it grew steadily larger as it approached. It had something, a dark shape, clutched in its claws.

She jumped to her feet, meaning to run to the highest parapet. But then she stopped herself. No, she would wait. She told herself. She wanted to hear what Nazar had to say at dinner tonight.

She waited. The servants arrived exactly on schedule and lit her room. One opened the door on the wardrobe and began to rummage about among all the dresses.

Rhi uttered a gasp of exasperation and throwing up her hands, left the room. She took herself to the dining hall where the king was waiting.

He looked at her and growled in disapproval. "Wrong attire and same clothes as last night!" he muttered.

Rhi shrugged and seated herself. A plate of roast mutton was set before her by a blank faced servant.

King Nazar glared at her and drummed his fingers in irritation. Rhi took no notice.

She looked at the meat as if she had never seen it before. "Sire, where do you get your meat?" she asked him suddenly.

He frowned. "That is an odd beginning to our dinner conversation," he stated.

Rhi raised her eyebrows and continued anyway.

"I'm just saying I've never seen any livestock or animals of any kind since I entered your kingdom. I was just wondering where the meat comes from."

Her eyes turned to the servant. "Are you feeding *them* to me?"

He followed her gaze and burst out in laughter. "Heavens no! What an absurd thought! I am no cannibal."

She smiled in return. "I'm glad to hear it."

The king shook his head and picked up his knife and fork. "The dragon brings me back game from the mountains surrounding my kingdom. Animals are still plentiful there."

He took a few bites. "I like meat. It makes one strong."

Rhi nodded. "So the dragon is like your hunter's falcon?"

He snorted in scorn. "Dragons are better than silly birds. Besides falcons can only eat other small birds and mice. No one crosses a dragon and they can eat whatever they choose to."

Rhi nodded again. She was beginning to understand why all the falcon plaques were smashed. "So this dragon is your…pet?"

The corners of his mouth twitched. "If you like."

Rhi took another bite of meat while she mulled this over. "And how long have you had this pet dragon?"

The question seemed to irritate him. "You know what I want to know is, what kind of woman doesn't want fine dresses and jewels?"

"Um, that would be me," she replied.

"Yes, but why? From the state I found you in, it's obvious you've never had a fine thing in your life. And yet you refuse my gifts of wealth? I might expect this from a woman who has been raised in finery and grown immune to it but not someone of your background. What is it that you really want?"

She lowered her knife and fork, knowing her answer would not please him. "A goodly horse and an open road before me. No more than that."

His eyes narrowed and he shook his head.

"Wanderling!" he said and sighed, disappointed. "You will not get those things here. You are on my land and in my castle. I own everything you see about you and the lands without. That means I own you as well."

He sighed and pushed his plate back, looking at her keenly.

"You are alive only because you have amused me so far. But I will tire of you soon enough like I tire of all things. And then I will expect you to obey me."

Ilis eyes turned to the empty faced servant who was refilling his wine glass.

"And you will obey me one way or another."

It was an unspoken threat.

Rhi felt like someone was starting to strangle her slowly.

"I know you spoke to Shayne today."

She tried not to look concerned but failed. Her eyes turned to the servants. His gaze followed her own.

"Yes, they told me. If you phrase the question properly, they have no choice but to give the correct response. They are incapable of deceit or lies."

His gaze turned back to her. "It makes no difference to me that you spoke to him. You can talk all you like to him. It won't help you. Neither of you is ever going to leave here."

Rhi swallowed with difficulty.

She felt her world was getting smaller and smaller with every word he said.

***

Rhi shivered in the predawn cold wind no matter how tightly she wrapped the heavy woolen cloak about her. It was very windy atop the highest parapet even though it was still summer.

She hadn't been able to sleep after her dinner with the king. Her mind was spinning so much with all the things which had been told to her. She could only catch sleep in brief snatches.

She hardly knew who or what to believe anymore. Maybe life as a simple farm girl *was* better. Maybe her decision to run away was a bit too hasty. If she had stayed at home and married Brody even if she didn't love him, she certainly wouldn't have had to deal with magic, and cruel kings who thought they could turn into dragons and such.

She took a deep breath of cold wind and shut her eyes. No, she told herself firmly. She had chosen this life with all its glories and perils and this was what fate had dealt her. Good or bad she had to look it in the eye and face whatever the challenge was. She had to believe the open road was still there waiting for her. If she could only figure out this one riddle, she could have her old lifestyle back once again. She just had to see this through somehow, some way.

Rhi sensed she was no longer so alone on the castle top. She opened her eyes and looked about. She huddled closer to the shadows in the pile of stone rubble she was hiding behind.

King Nazar had stepped out from behind a wooden door which led to the top parapet. One look in his face and Rhi knew he did not suspect her presence. He never glanced her way, or looked to the right or left. He just strode to the claw marks in the stone and climbing up, stood on the very edge of the parapet's lip looking down, so far down, at the ground far below. His red cloak billowed out behind him as the wind caught it like wings, his black hair was tousled by the rough gusts.

The first rays of the morning sun broke over the horizon and lit his body up in a golden fire. Rhi blinked. No, she wasn't dreaming. King Nazar had burst suddenly into golden flames! He raised his head and faced the dawning sun. His dark eyes had become red faceted gems which glittered and flashed, returning the sun's brilliant rays. Wide-eyed in disbelief, Rhi watched as his skin began to ripple like ocean waves and red, reptilian scales erupted out of the goose-bumps of his skin, like a cat's retractable claws. Nazar reached out his arms as if to embrace the sun. As he reached out, his red cloak swept forward and attached to the back of his arms and their composition changed from flapping cloth to fibrous red skin. His fingers lengthened and melded with the forming wings like a bat's webbed fingers.

Nazar cried out, a cry which resembled some weird blend of lion's roar and eagle's scream. It was so loud it made the rocks tremble and Rhi clapped her hands over her ears. Then Nazar just seemed to faint and allowed himself to fall forward into the wind and off of the parapet. Down he fell out of Rhi's line of vision. She stood up so as not to lose sight of him. She blinked twice against the harsh wind in her eyes.

An enormous, red golden dragon was beneath her, hovering, glowing with new magic in the air right below her parapet. It reached out its long, red armored neck and gaped its cavernous maw filled with spear-like teeth and cried aloud again. Then its wings flapped downwards once pushing its great bulk away from the castle and knocking Rhi end over end in the rush of wind from its wings.

She looked up to see the enormous reptilian shape quickly grow small in the sky as it raced away from the castle on its morning rounds.

Rhi collapsed in shock on the cold rock of the parapet's walkway.

SHAYNE'S STORY

"So you are a prince and your brother can turn into a dragon."

It was a statement from Rhi to Shayne, not a question.

Shayne nodded as he greedily gulped the water from the skin she had brought him.

"I think you now need to tell me about your family. I will not take no for an answer," she told him.

She seated herself comfortably on the floor next to the iron bars of his prison cell.

Shayne considered her as he tore off some hunks of bread and hungrily consumed them as if he hadn't eaten in weeks although it had really only been a few days.

"You saw him turn into a dragon?" he inquired between bites.

She nodded wordlessly. "How does that happen? Did an evil sorcerer enchant him or a witch curse him?"

Shayne laughed. "Were it was all that simple! Then there would be a good person needing to be rescued underneath. But no, he did that to himself. He wanted to become a dragon. He always did dream about dragons."

His gaze drifted off into the black space of the darkness around him. He then jarred himself back to the present and turned back to her with an apologetic smile.

"Remember when I told you our family had elf blood?"

She nodded.

"Well that's the part I lied the most about," he told her shrugging helplessly. "Many generations ago, one of the princesses of my family met and fell in love with an elfin suitor. My ancestors welcomed him with open arms, believing him to be a prince who had fallen out of favor with his family."

Here in the story Shayne grinned mockingly. "He was no kind of a prince! If only they had known," he sighed sadly. "The elf suitor was no one in particular, in fact most elves shunned him like the plague and wouldn't even admit they knew of him. I wish they had been more forthcoming. You see he was just a common elf but much more, he was a thief, a vagabond and a willful murderer. My grandmother, many times removed, did not learn the truth until she had already borne him several children. When she discovered who he really was, she sent the children away for safekeeping and then confronted him. He killed her in cold blood. Then he went searching for his estranged children. He was caught and put to death long before it ever happened and my family thought that was the end of the matter. But it wasn't."

His voice lapsed into silence and he stared blankly off into space while his hands busied themselves with tearing off a chunk of cheese.

"From generation to generation there has been something wrong with the children of my family, something which has been passed down in the bloodstream to this day. Sometimes it's no more than magic flows easily to them and through them."

"Like your ability to talk to horses?" Rhi interjected.

Shayne nodded. "Yes, exactly. But then there is the flipside of the coin. There are children in my family who just act wrong no matter how well they are raised,"

Here Rhi's brow wrinkled in confusion. "How do you mean 'wrong'? How can a child act 'wrong'?"

He sighed and paused eating. "Certain children in our family seem to be very fascinated with violent acts and bloodletting. And no amount of scolding or gentle nurturing seemed to be able to guide them to the right path. Take Nazar for example. All during our childhood together, he was very competitive. No matter what I did, Nazar had to do the same thing bigger and better. He was always vying for my father's affection. I seemed to be the favorite and Nazar was insanely jealous of this fact. I didn't understand why then but I think I understand better now."

He took another hasty gulp from the wineskin, wiped his mouth with a sleeve and continued. "Nazar was the firstborn, so this meant he was first in line to the throne. His life was already planned out for him. But me being the second-borne, meant I could live a somewhat freer lifestyle if I so chose. I had the heart of a wanderling. I wanted to renounce the throne and live life on the road, traveling and exploring the many lands about me."

"Wanderling…" Rhi repeated softly remembering Nazar had said the name to her the night before. She remembered more the tone of voice he had used when he said it; one of disgust, ridicule and utter revulsion.

"What is a 'wanderling' exactly?" she asked.

Shayne smiled gently at her. "A wanderling is an adventurer or an explorer, a sword for hire. They live by their own rules and follow their own laws. Their code of ethics is very high and it is not wise to cross them. Their only master is the open road. I am a wanderling."

Rhi smiled, happy to hear he shared her dream of the open road.

"My father always wanted to do that too but he couldn't. He was the king. He had responsibilities which could not be ignored. He had a kingdom to rule. He could not just up and leave for adventure on the road. I could but he could not."

Shayne rubbed his eyes. "Nazar never saw it quite like that. He just saw it as whatever I did, father fawned all over me and when he did the same thing his response was somewhat…shall we say…muted. Receiving this response made Nazar insane with jealousy."

Shayne sighed heavily and closed his eyes in pain. "Nazar was never 'right', even as a child. There was always something wrong about him, something twisted and dark. Too much of the dark elf's blood. I got the good part of the magic, he inherited all the bad."

Shayne rubbed his face and forced himself to continue. "I never wanted to compete with him. I was just being me. But Nazar turned everything into a competition. He saw everything I did and said as a sign of weakness from me. And it got worse as we matured to the point where I began to avoid him like the servants did. He only saw this as an act of cowardice and would purposely hunt me out to torment me.

"I began to take long trips into the countryside to get away from him. I would travel everywhere within this kingdom, often in disguise so people wouldn't treat me any different. I loved the land and its people, from lowly farmer to highest noble. I just didn't love my brother.

"It was easy for most people not to love Nazar. He tormented the castle staff mercilessly. All while I was gone, I was relieved I didn't have to deal with him. But I also felt guilty because I realized the castle servants didn't have such luxury. They *had* to deal with him every day of their life. Every time I came home, it seemed I always had to rescue one of the servants from his vicious tongue and brutal hand. I could not be everywhere at once and neither could my poor father who was growing grayer day by day in the struggle to manage both his kingdom and his cruel son. People whispered there would be a bad end of it someday. Oh how right they were!"

Here his voice lapsed into silence and his eyes stared blankly off into the distance. He was still for so long, Rhi almost believed he had turned into one of the castle servants, blank faced, empty and soulless.

Rhi crept closer to him. Quietly she reached through the bars and laid a sympathetic hand on his arm.

"Shayne?" she whispered.

He didn't stir. He continued to stare blankly off into space but he began to speak again, moving on with the story of his life.

"I came home from one of my trips to find my brother drunk and beating a serving girl until she could no longer see. I fought him off of her, an easy task when your adversary is so disgustingly drunk. I ordered the castle guards to lock him in his quarters until he sobered up. I then took the serving girl to her quarters and doctored her wounds myself. I did my best to console her parents this would not happen again. It didn't. But what happened next was worse, so much worse."

Shayne uttered a soft noise which sounded like a sob and turned his face away. Rhi pressed closer. He held up a hand begging for patience.

"The next night I was having dinner in the main feast hall with my father and some other distinguished guests when my brother arrived, late for dinner and drunker than I have ever seen him. He came blasting into the hall, rude as a troll and smelly as an ogre and proceeded to blame me in front of all gathered of crime after crime. I literally jumped over the feast hall table to silence his claims and we tussled right there. Drunk as he was, he was much bigger and stronger than I and landed a lucky shot which dazed me into helplessness for the next few moments. While I lay on the feast hall floor, my vision spinning crazily, he rushed our father and stabbed him to the heart. My father was dead before he hit the floor."

Rhi covered her mouth in shock.

"And that's what really happened?"

Shayne glanced back to her. His eyes were glassy and very tired looking.

"I know he told you I killed my father. But I didn't. Nazar has no memory of that night. He was too drunk to remember anything. I know it is his word against mine, but this is really what happened. And I will tell you or anyone else the exact same story a million times over until someone believes it. My brother killed our father in a drunken fit. Nazar remembers nothing of the incident. So, of course, I had to be the culprit."

There was a long silence between them.

"What happened next, in the kingdom I mean?"

Shayne shrugged. "The impossible. Nazar was crowned king."

Rhi gasped in horror. "What? How is it even possible? He wasn't punished in any way whatsoever?"

Shayne shrugged. "Well, something like this had never happened before. There was no contingency plan in case the king died before his time and his successor was not fit to rule. The kingdom was without a king. And Nazar was next in line for the throne. The coronation was quick. The land had to have a king, even a crazy one."

"Where were you in all this?" she asked.

Shayne's face grew dark and he receded. His emotional shield went up again. She almost expected him not to tell her what had happened and just avoid the issue altogether.

But tell her he did. "I ran away like a coward."

"What? Why?" she asked.

He hung his head in regret. "Because I didn't want to be king."

Rhi just stared at him. "But…look here. I'm just a simple farm girl and I don't know what I'm talking about but it seems to me the next step would be to muster an army, which knowing how people despised your brother, probably would have been very easy, and challenge him for claim to the throne."

A small smile flickered briefly across Shayne's face. "My dear you may be 'just a simple farm girl' as you put it but you understand the matter well enough. Yes, that is exactly what I should have done. But I didn't. I ran away before Nazar was even crowned. Because I was afraid of being king. And challenging my brother's claim to the throne also meant I might have to kill him. And somehow killing one's sibling no matter how wrong and irredeemable they are, just didn't seem right to me. I really don't want to be a kinslayer in any way whatsoever. I don't want that on my conscience."

Rhi was silent for a moment mulling over his story. She still couldn't get past the fact he ran away when his kingdom needed him the most. "If you had to do it over again, would you still have run away?"

Shayne sighed, crossed his arms in front of his chest, frowned and thought hard. "I have considered this question many times because my actions back then have caused me a lot of regret and guilt since then. I think I would challenge his right to the throne. I think I would raise an army. But I would also try not to kill him. I would move heaven and earth to avoid that outcome. It is never right to kill your own brother even if he has have done everything to deserve it. That is just not the right punishment from me to him."

His words redeemed himself in Rhi's mind somewhat. Shayne did have blood on his hands; the blood of every common person in this land who needed salvation from their king and didn't get it. At least he had the conscience to regret his decision even if it was too late to do anything about it.

"And...how does the dragon play into all this?"

Shayne rubbed his face. "That's where everything gets a little murky. I was away from the castle so by the time I heard any news, it had been passed down the gossip chain and gotten very convoluted. Word among the people was soon after his coronation, Nazar hired on a 'court wizard'. Nazar wanted to learn how to work magic to strengthen his hold on his new kingdom. The gossip matched with my personal experience growing up with my brother. He was always fascinated by magic things, good or bad. But this particular wizard had a cloudy reputation. It seemed he liked to mix white magic with black to get more power out of his spells. Doing this is walking a slippery slope. Nazar didn't care. This was just the kind of thing he gravitated to. Then all of a sudden, the wizard disappeared."

Rhi sat up straighter. "Why? What do you think happened?"

Shayne gave her a smug look which hinted at nothing good. "Knowing my brother, Nazar learned what he wanted from him and then killed him. That sounds like just the kind of thing he would do."

"Outside the castle, word had gotten out their new king was crazy. People were packing up and leaving the kingdom, fearing for their lives and the lives of their families. As some left, their relatives inherited their taxes so they had double the taxes to pay. This only pushed more people to leave.

"People everywhere in this kingdom saw the writing on the wall. The king could not be trusted to take care of his people. The politics of the land were about to implode. Leave now or be swept up in the destruction which would follow.

"Then word came from the castle the king needed new staff. There were rumors the only reason he needed them was the old staff were mysteriously disappearing at an alarming rate."

A shiver of ice went down Rhi's back. "What was he doing?" she whispered. She was afraid of the answer.

"Experimenting with his new found skills. He needed 'volunteers'!" Shayne replied.

Rhi shuddered in dread.

"Then word got around the king was redecorating the castle. All my family's plaques were being torn down and smashed."

"The falcon!" Rhi suddenly cried out. "Your family sign was the falcon!"

Shayne grinned widely and nodded. "Nazar never liked the symbol. He always liked dragons. He wanted father to give him a pet dragon for his birthday. Every year for quite some time he begged for a pet dragon. I forget when he stopped asking. I concluded the plaques and the missing staff had something to do with this dream. He was trying to catch a dragon."

Rhi's face wrinkled in confusion. "Can you actually do that? Get a pet dragon?"

Shayne laughed. "No!" he chuckled. "But you can trap one. This is what I think he's done, found a dragon and trapped it. The missing staff were just practice. He was practicing taking their souls out of their bodies and trapping them so he could do what he wanted with their forms. It didn't work with humans. You remove a person's soul and their body dies. But all these servants are frozen at the point just before death, therefore still somewhat useful to Nazar, unspeaking and uncomplaining."

"And it is magically possibly to ensnare a dragon this way?"

Shayne frowned and sucked his teeth. "Not exactly. Nazar was able to remove the dragon's spirit and trap it in something. Then he could inhabit the dragon's body for a short time, say from dusk to dawn."

"What about at night? Does the dragon body get its spirit back?" she asked.

He shook his head.

"If the dragon ever got its spirit back in its body where it belongs, then this castle would be leveled to the ground. Dragons do not like to be caged!"

"And what if the dragon was freed?" Rhi suggested.

"Everything and everyone in this castle including you, me and Nazar would be burned to a crisp. Probably. Dragons do not handle captivity well."

Rhi thought hard, chewing her lip. "But it also might not. It might just go after Nazar."

Shayne shook his head. "My dear, that is one mighty big *IF*!"

She grabbed the bars of the cell tightly. "Freeing this dragon might just be the only way to save you and me. I'm not becoming one of his soulless slaves and I'm not marrying him. I'm willing to risk it. Are you?"

Shayne gazed into the details of her face for a moment. He reached through the bars and stroked her cheek. "I'm tired of being a coward. This isn't much of a chance but I'll take it. I'd rather die burned to a crisp than to run from another fight I should have faced and didn't."

Rhi pulled back away from him and smiled. "You still have one lie to make good on," she said.

He raised his eyebrows. "And that is?"

"I know you know what the inscription on the medallion says. Tell me."

Shayne took a deep breath and nodded. He reached out and picked up the medallion from where it swung about her neck, flipped it over and read it to himself in the dim flickering light of the torch.

"This is the emblem of the children of my family. Every child is given one on their eighth birthday. Children in my family are called 'feathers' in the old language of the realm until their coming of age. And the inscription on the back of the medallion is magic, it changes for each one who wears it. This one reads:

"Falcon born with wanderling heart,
Wanderling born with falcon heart,
Two souls with one true goal,
To let it be and to live free."

His eyes met hers. "I knew the day long ago when you named your horse 'Falcon' that you would be important. I just didn't know how much."

The Dragon

Rhi's next thought was to find where Nazar had hidden his "pet" dragon. But she was quickly running out of daylight. She wanted to go looking for the dragon immediately. Instead she had to turn her mind to her obligatory dinner date with Nazar.

She returned to her room, her thoughts spinning. She requested a change of clothes from her night servant making sure she gave clear instructions the attire was to be male. The servant nodded and returned with the requested clothes. They were the garments of a man but they also had the embellishments of royalty, dark velvet with bright metallic trim. Rhi sighed and gave in. It seemed if she insisted on wearing a man's clothes, Nazar was determined she would not wear commoner threads.

Before she left her room, she hailed the servant who had brought her the clothes. He faced her and awaited her command. She looked him up and down, considering her next words carefully.

"Do you know where Nazar keeps his dragon?" she asked.

The servant blinked once and then shook his head in denial.

Rhi sighed in frustration and ran a hand through her hair. She thought harder. They could only answer yes, or no so she had to be very specific.

"Does any of the staff know where he keeps his dragon or how to get there?"

The servant blinked twice, hesitated and then nodded.

Rhi's eyes narrowed. No servant had ever hesitated before responding.

"Bring this man to me at once," she ordered.

Again the servant blinked twice, hesitated and then left. Soon after he left there was a gentle rap on the door.

She told the servant to enter.

A middle-aged woman with black hair and hazel eyes stepped in and stood awaiting her command.

Rhi did not expect it to be a woman.

They just stood regarding each other for a long moment.

Rhi then remembered she had to tell her something. She cleared her throat loudly.

"Thank you. You may return to your duties."

The woman did not blink but curtseyed and did as she was bid.

Rhi immediately left her room and made her way through the many hallways of the castle to the great feast hall.

She stepped into the feast hall and stopped.

Nazar was there in his customary place at the head of the table. But behind him, lined up along the wall were five of the loveliest women Rhi had ever laid eyes on. They all wore fine dresses of five different colors and were dripping with expensive jewels which flashed at the slightest ray of light as if they were lit with an inner fire.

But their skin was colorless and their eyes empty, devoid of spirit just like every other person who occupied the castle.

Rhi bit her lip in worry. It seemed Nazar had ulterior motives for her to wear fine clothes. The suspicion made Rhi tremble in dread.

Nazar was narrowly looking her up and down. He was still frowning but this time he nodded.

"Not a gown but it will do," he said gruffly.

Rhi took a deep breath and steeled herself against what was to come. She seated herself at the setting by his side.

"But sire!" she said in mock surprise. "It's still the wrong attire."

Nazar scowled at her attempt for humor.

"My dear, you would be lovely in rags! But I must demand certain appropriate attire for the feast hall. This seems to be a workable compromise."

He seated himself and waved for the servant to serve them.

"I'm glad we can come to an agreement on something," she replied.

He nodded as he sipped from his glass.

For some reason, Rhi didn't seem to have much of an appetite. Her eyes kept returning to the five women who stood motionless as statues behind the king, their blank eyes staring off into space.

Nazar seemed amused by her attention to them. She could sense he was smugly waiting for her to ask the inevitable question.

She struggled with how to breech the subject, knowing all the while he would turn her words against her.

"Sire, shouldn't you introduce me to your guests?" she finally asked against her will.

The corners of his mouth twitched. "No. If they had souls I would," he replied. "But they have no souls. Therefore they are nobody. They're not really people anymore."

Rhi took another deep breath. "Then what is the purpose of their presence, Sire?"

He smiled. He was enjoying every moment of this! She wanted to slap the smile right off of his face. "They are here as reminders only. Reminders of what happens to people who say no to me."

Rhi swallowed carefully. "If they refused your advances then they are brave women indeed."

Nazar's fist suddenly hit the table with such a force the dinnerware clattered. Rhi jumped nearly out of her skin and dropped her knife in fright.

"*NO ONE* has any right to refuse anything I order them to do! I am the king! What I say is law!"

Rhi took three deep breaths before she could trust her voice to speak again. "Then why go through all the trouble of asking anybody anything? If what you want is what you want, why don't you just order it instead of asking?"

The question seemed to surprise him. He sat back in his great chair considering her for a moment.

"I asked the first three women to marry me. They refused. I even gave them plenty of time to consider their decision. They still refused. I ordered the next one to marry me, told her she had no choice. She still refused me. The last one just wouldn't give me an answer. I got tired of waiting and took what I wanted from her."

He sighed. "The question I have for you, is which woman will you be? I want you to marry me. Will you say yes, or no?"

The question she had dreaded had been put to her.

The food turned to sand in her throat. Her heart was pounding in her chest. She remembered what Shayne had said to her earlier, her time was short when he proposed marriage. She fought not to let it rattle her composure. She had to stall him somehow.

"Why do you even want to marry me?" she asked. "I'm no princess! I'm just a farm girl. You've got five women here who will do whatever you say. Why do you need me?" she managed to choke back the tears of fear as she blurted this out.

He sipped his wine slowly, rolling it around on his tongue as he assembled the answer as if he had all the time in the world, and he did. His next words staggered her.

"Shayne loves you."

Rhi gasped several times before she could trust her own voice. "He hasn't said anything to me about it."

Nazar laughed. "Because he's a coward, that's why! Most men are when it comes to facing the woman of their dreams. Shayne has always been yellow-bellied when it comes to women. But he's never taken to any woman like he's taken to you and I want to know why. That's why you're going to marry me. Or you're going to be the sixth woman in the line."

She looked at the five women assembled behind him. They hadn't moved since she walked into the feast hall. Rhi wondered what their names were, where they had come from, what their dreams were, did their families worry about them or were they dead too? There were so many blank pages in the book of their lives. Now they were caught living this un-life, in servitude to a master who could have cared less about the little details of their lives, paused in the seconds before their own death, not dead but not alive either. They were trapped in a cage; blank, empty, unreal, uncaring and unable to dream. Not a real life at all. All the people in this castle needed a knight to come riding up on his white horse and save them.

But the white knight wasn't coming because he didn't exist.

"So my dear, what's it going to be? Will you marry me or no?"

Rhi coughed trying to force her voice to return. "I...I...don't know. I have to think about it," she rasped out finally in a very small, little voice.

Her eyes looked up and met those of the unseeing women. She found herself transfixed, unable to look away.

Nazar growled, not happy with her answer. "Fine! Be that way! Think about it. But do not think too long. I am not a patient man."

In a fog, Rhi stood up, curtseyed and carefully walked out of the feast hall. Once out of line of the king's vision, she fled as fast as her feet could carry her through the hallways, up the stairs to her room. She slammed and locked the door behind her and fell breathless on the bed.

For the thousandth time she wished she was somewhere else.

***

Rhi awoke to the roar of dragon wings outside her bedroom window. She sat up straight in fright. The dragon hovered in front of her window, looking in. Then it uttered a huge, reptilian laugh which made her bedposts shudder and flew away.

She remembered the night before.

Nazar had asked her to marry him.

"When he asks you to marry him, your time is short." Shayne had said.

She felt cold inside.

There was a gentle rap on her door and a servant came in bearing a silver tray with her breakfast. She found herself unable to take her eyes off of his blank, staring face.

She did not want to become like all the other soulless people in the castle. There had to be some way out of this predicament.

She thought about her conversation with Shayne the day before.

She had to find out where Nazar had hidden the dragon. It was a slim chance but a slim chance was better than no chance at all.

She seated herself and ate her breakfast as she thought. When she had finished, she hailed the servant who had brought her the tray and requested he bring her the woman from the night before. While she waited, she quickly changed out of her dressing gown into her breeches, boots and tunic with a vest. She was brushing and braiding her long hair when the woman stepped into her room and stood waiting.

Before she remembered, she had asked, "What is your name?"

But the woman curtseyed and gestured with two fingers on one hand to her eyes.

Rhi stood there blinking in confusion for a moment.

"Hazel?" she asked finally and the woman nodded.

Rhi smiled broadly, pleased with herself. At least she had managed to figure out somebody's name!

"Hazel, do you know where Nazar keeps his dragon?" she asked.

Hazel pointed out the window.

Rhi frowned and stomped her foot in frustration.

"No! I know the dragon is gone," she growled to herself and thought hard as to how to phrase the question. "I mean where does he keep the dragon during the day? Where does he have the spirit trapped?"

Hazel cocked her head to the side like a curious dog.

Rhi sighed again in frustration. She didn't understand.

Or so she thought.

Hazel took hold of her arm abruptly and gestured for her to follow. Then she turned and left the bedchamber. Rhi followed wordlessly.

Hazel led her through a maze of passages to an enormous bedroom three times the size of Rhi's own chamber. Rhi just stood and stared at the murals on the walls and ceiling of hunting scenes and the gilded molding climbing up the corners of the walls like tree branches to the ceiling above. The room was so opulent and rich it amazed her any one person could feel comfortable in it.

"Is this Nazar's bedroom?" she asked.

Hazel nodded.

The serving woman was standing next to a full-length mirror.

"And where does he keep the dragon?" she asked.

Hazel pointed to the mirror.

"The dragon is in the mirror?" Rhi asked.

Hazel shook her head in denial.

Rhi came up to stand in front of the mirror.

"I don't understand."

Hazel reached out and grabbed her hand and shoved it *into* the mirror. Rhi gasped in fright for instead of her hand meeting glass, it went through the mirror as if through a doorway.

Rhi snatched her hand back in shock and examined it. Yes, it was her hand and it was whole and unharmed. She looked to Hazel. The serving maid nodded encouragingly.

Apparently Rhi was to step through the mirror.

She looked at her reflection and took a deep breath. Then she closed her eyes and stepped into the mirror.

She felt like she had stepped through a pane of water except she wasn't wet. It seemed to cling to her and yet it released her gently.

Rhi blinked. It was darker here on the other side of the mirror. She had the feeling she was standing in a room much larger than the one she had left. She could hear water dripping and feel small gusts of wind buffet her lightly. She gazed about and suddenly gasped in wonder.

She found she was standing in a huge cavern encrusted in crystal. The walls, the roof above her head, everything was glittering and faceted in every color imaginable.

And then the crystals began to flash and shine with a light from within as if they were alive. The cavern grew brighter with the flickering of these lights.

She suddenly became aware there was a presence in the cavern. Rhi felt like she was standing in the center of a room in a mansion haunted by hundreds of ghosts, ghosts who were suddenly aware of her and watching her with unfriendly eyes.

She was abruptly knocked to the floor with the force of a tumultuous sound. It was the clamor of hundreds of voices screaming. She could hear them inside and outside her head. She clamped her hands over her ears but the screams only grew louder, deafening her with the strength of their sound.

"Stop it! Stop it!" she screamed back into the din but her voice was drowned out by the cacophony about her.

And then there came another sound. It sounded like falling boulders in the mountains. It was louder than the screams. Suddenly all was quiet and still. The many voices had ceased and were now waiting, waiting for her to say something momentous.

The sound of boulders came again and this time Rhi realized it was a voice.

"What is this?" said the mighty voice. "You are not Nazar!"

Rhi looked up trembling but could not see anyone or any creature who belonged to the voice. "I certainly am not Nazar!" she managed to gasp out. "I am...."

But the great voice cut her off. "No!" it said. "Do not speak your name! For names are an evil made only to ensnare. Names should not exist."

Rhi climbed carefully to her feet. "Are you too a prisoner of Nazar? Did he catch you with your name?" she asked the air before her.

The unseen entity made a sound like hot water hissing on cold stones. "Yes, that was how he caught me. But how did you earn such charity from him for I see your soul and your body are still one?"

It was Rhi's turn to grumble. "Apparently not for long though. If I do not give him the answer he desires, he will separate me from my soul."

The hundred voices softly began to moan in pain about her.

"What is that?" she asked.

The moaning made her bones shiver.

"That is the sound of Nazar's poor servants. Their souls wail at their injustice," replied the great voice who did not want to be named.

"But..." stammered Rhi, not understanding. "I thought they were all dead."

The voice seemed to chuckle. "Not yet. Not quite," it answered. "They were frozen in time an instant before their death. They are not alive and yet they are unable to die. So they scream and moan and wail here in this cavern. Unquiet, restless spirits trapped here with me. Forever."

Rhi took a few tentative steps toward the source of the voice. "Then...can they be returned to their bodies?" she asked.

The voice laughed, a sad laugh full of regret. "My dear, if they could be returned to their bodies to live or die, do you not think I would have already done it by now?"

Rhi smiled as understanding finally dawned on her. "Not if you are without your body just as they are," she replied. "You're the dragon aren't you?"

Again the rumbling came followed by a hiss like a million angry snakes. "You are very perceptive for such a young thing."

Rhi looked about her at the ceiling of the cavern. "Nazar trapped the souls of his people in this crystal, correct?" she asked.

The voice rumbled and boomed before her. "Yes, that is so."

"Then...if he must have a solid vessel to trap the soul in...then where is your cage?"

The voice chuckled, echoing all about her. "You are approaching it," it replied. "I will ask the other souls to increase their light so you might see."

A soft, red glow issued from the crystal overhead. As the light increased, Rhi saw a shape standing in a shaft of clear light in the direct center of the room. It looked to be an enormous stone egg.

"There. Better?"

"Yes..." Rhi breathed. She stared at the stone egg in wonder. It was dark in color but streaked with red and black branches across it like veins. The egg was lit from within by a yellow, glowing light.

Rhi reached out and touched the egg. It felt as hard as polished marble but it was warm to the touch. It stood just a little taller than her and was supported by a pedestal with words carved on it, words in a language Rhi could not read.

"What does the inscription say? I cannot read it," she asked.

The dragon's voice laughed. "No one but Nazar can read it. It is in an ancient tongue secret to all but the most learned of wizards."

She bit her lip in worry. "But you can read it, can't you?" Rhi said urgently.

"Of course I can read it!" sniffed the dragon. "There is no tongue ancient or recent, that the youngest of my kind cannot speak and read. Your writing is pathetically simple for my kin to decipher."

The dragon paused. "It is a riddle. It will not rhyme once translated into your words. But it is said to hold the key to breaking the spell which holds me caged in the stone."

Her heart leapt in hope. "Then out with it!" Rhi demanded. "And let's be done with all this cruelty Nazar has created!"

"You won't be able to figure it out," the dragon's voice dared her.

Rhi snarled in frustration and balled her hands into fists. "Look here dragon!" she said angrily. "According to my understanding, I have very little time until I join the other spirits trapped in crystal. Now you give me the key to unlock this mystery and you dismiss me without even trying? Maybe you haven't been caged long enough."

The dragon growled and the room trembled violently.

But Rhi was not frightened this time.

"Tell me the inscription! Let me at least try to save myself. Maybe I can save you, too."

The light inside the egg twisted and turned. There was a great scraping noise as of scales grating on rocks.

"You would save a dragon who might kill you once released?"

Rhi laid her hands on the stone egg before her. "Why not? You're caged. So am I. We both hate it equally. We both want to be free. Why shouldn't I help someone with the same curse as myself? Who better understands being trapped than you and I right now?"

The dragon rumbled in indecision.

"What have you got to lose? Come on, dragon, take a chance."

There was an enormous hiss. "Very well. I will tell you the inscription. And if you can manage it, you will free me along with yourself. And when I am free, I will kill Nazar."

"Agreed!" she answered immediately. Rhi knelt down at the base of the stone egg and traced the foreign letters with her fingers as the dragon recited them for her.

"The inscription reads as follows:

> The falcon's cry will lay low the lies
> Through blood, a bond is shared
> Wanderling's choice
> Destiny's sacrifice
> The stones will scream,
> Blood will stream
> Chains will be broken,
> Doors will be open
> Dragon chained will fly free again."

There was a deep, stony grumble from the dragon.

"See? It makes no sense at all, except for the last line about me."

Rhi was chewing her lip and shaking her head. "No, pardon me dragon, but you're wrong," she said as she thought. "*'Wanderling's choice'*? This could mean me. I'm a wanderling. But what is the choice?"

There was another hiss. "You understand some of this?" The dragon's voice was actually beginning to sound excited.

"The falcon means the family who inhabited the castle before. Their symbol was the falcon," Rhi muttered as she thought.

"*'Falcon's cry will lay low the lies'* I don't understand that part," the dragon said.

Rhi knew exactly what it was referring to but she held back from saying anything.

"*'Through blood, a bond is shared,'*" she muttered. "What does that mean? Someone of a certain bloodline?"

The dragon grumbled thinking. "What is your bloodline, child?" it spoke to her.

Rhi shrugged.

"Me? Well, I'm just a farmer's daughter," she said.

"Hmmm," rumbled the dragon. "Has your family always been farmers?"

The question completely took Rhi aback for a moment. "I…don't know. I suppose so. I only know to my grandparents. Are you suggesting there might be blue blood in my family further back?"

The dragon chuckled. "Perhaps. Anything is possible."

Rhi had no idea how to respond. "But there's no way to know that."

The dragon chuckled.

Rhi coughed. "All right. How do I find that out?"

For a third time the dragon chuckled.

"To answer the question, I will need one drop of your blood placed on the surface of the stone egg. A dragon can always sense what is in the blood of a person."

Rhi stepped back in shock. Now the dragon was asking for her to cut herself. "Is this really necessary?" she asked in a tiny voice.

The dragon seemed to be enjoying this. "How much do you like having your spirit in its house of flesh?"

Rhi blinked. She began to look about her. On the floor of the cavern, she found a pile of stone shards. She picked out what looked to be a very sharp piece and returned to the stone egg.

"I hope you're right!" she said and then she took a deep breath, gritted her teeth against the pain and pricked her finger with the sharp point of the broken shale. A large drop of deep red blood welled up through the small wound on her skin. She pressed the drop against the surface of the stone egg.

The dragon made a sound like a satisfied cat's purr. "*'Through blood, a bond is shared,'*" murmured the dragon in quiet delight.

At the exact instant, Rhi realized what she had done. She felt the mistake she had made. Something intruded into her being, pushing her core aside and sharing space with it. Suddenly her body was home to two souls, her own and now the dragon's.

"You lied to me!" she shouted. She let go of the stone, balled her hands into fists again and began to pound on the stone egg.

"How dare you! I did not give you permission. Get out of me this instant!"

The dragon laughed its reply to her. "No," was all it said.

Rhi wailed in horror. She wasn't sure which was worse, the prospect of being robbed of her soul or having to house another soul which wasn't her own.

"Why?" she cried and fell sobbing to her knees.

"Because I am a dragon. And I must survive in any way that's possible to me. You provided an opportunity. Your naiveté gave me access to a living body. I will not deprive you of your soul because I wouldn't deign to copy the same tactic as my enemy. But to achieve my freedom and revenge I need a physical form and since my own has been stolen from me, yours will do nicely."

Rhi had collapsed sobbing onto the floor before the egg.

But the dragon's voice continued to mutter as it now had access to her thoughts and memories.

"*'Falcon's cry will lay low the lies.'* Ah! Now I understand. You have a lover."

She hiccupped helplessly. "He's not my lover. Why does everyone say he is?"

The dragon purred.

"Because a love between two people yet unspoken is still love nevertheless."

The dragon was silent for a long moment.

Rhi managed to control her sobbing and dashed the tears away. "Am I your slave now?"

The question seemed to startle the dragon.

"Hmmm. Slave," repeated the dragon slowly as it considered the words. "It is a harsh word, 'slave'. No, I do not want you to be my slave. Not after what I've been going through. I am, however, very interested in acquiring a spy. I'm sorry I had to force this upon you but I could not take the chance you might say no. I will not ask your forgiveness. Dragons have no use for human forgiveness. I will humbly beg you to allow me to eavesdrop on your conversations with Nazar. Perhaps I may discover something which will benefit both of us."

Rhi sniffed and said in a very small voice, "You could have asked permission."

The dragon rumbled knowingly. "No, I could not. And you know that very well."

Rhi forced her mind away from what she was feeling to concentrate on the job at hand and thought more about the inscription.

"*'Wanderling's choice, destiny's sacrifice'...*" she repeated. "Then shouldn't you be free now? I made a choice and a sacrifice."

The dragon only laughed louder. "You gave me a gift, not a sacrifice!" it replied.

"Yes, one you tricked me into, I might add!" Rhi said with some heat.

The dragon only continued to laugh. "My dear, do you even know the meaning of the word 'sacrifice'? It means to give up something. Not a gift or a meal or even a drop of blood. It means to give up something which before you had no intention of giving up, something you don't want to give up ever. But you do it for the greater good, because it's the right thing to do. And it's hard and it hurts a whole lot and you usually don't get anything out of it. But everyone else does. That's a sacrifice. And that's what you have yet to make: a great sacrifice."

"And what must I sacrifice?" she asked.

The dragon gave a long, drawn out sigh. "This only you can answer. Be assured you will know it when the time comes."

***

Rhi was breathless when she showed up in the dungeon with food and drink for Shayne.

"What's happened?" he asked and then he peered intently into her face. "What's wrong with your eyes?"

"Hello, prince!" boomed the dragon's voice right above their heads.

Shayne jumped back against the wall in shock. His eyes darted about the room, searching for the source of the voice.

Rhi hissed in irritation. "I told you not to do that! Can't I have a conversation with him in private?"

The dragon only chuckled in amusement.

"Rhi, what just happened? Who is that?" Shayne asked.

"I am the dragon. I now share this vessel. This means I can talk to whoever I wish, however I wish."

Shayne's gaze went back to Rhi. She shrugged apologetically. "Apparently I now have two souls, my own and the dragon's. It's a little crowded in here."

Shayne blinked several times as he digested this new bit of information. "And…how is it possible?"

"It tricked me. Look. That's not what I'm here to talk about. I need to know something and I wanted no interruptions!" she growled with an angry backward glance over her shoulder.

The dragon purred. "She wants to know about name magic. And if that is the case then you need to talk to both of us," the dragon's voice answered.

Rhi sighed and put her head in her hands. "This is going to get very confusing!" she muttered.

Shayne relaxed somewhat and sat down on the cold, stone floor, turning his attention back to Rhi and the food. "I'm listening. Ask away," he said uneasily.

"Well, why is it I don't have a soul name?"

"You're a commoner," both Shayne and the dragon said at once.

Shayne bowed to the air and motioned the dragon to continue as he tore off a hunk of bread. The dragon spoke as he ate.

"Soul names are a practice of the bluebloods. Common people never adopted the custom. Their call names *are* their soul names."

Rhi nodded as she took this in. "Do different family members know each other's soul names?" she went on.

Shayne nodded and spoke around a mouthful. "Usually. Nazar has known mine and I have always known his."

"Then all I have to do is find out Nazar's soul name?"

"No!" they both responded.

"It's not simple." Shayne went on. "Nazar has spent many years in magic study. Trapping someone with his soul name is a very complicated thing."

Here the dragon sniffed in derision. "For humans maybe. All that is required to ensnare someone is to say the name with clear mental intent to do so."

It was here Shayne had to interrupt. "That's how you *control* someone by using their soul name. But Nazar does more than control. He has separated the soul from the body. That's high magic. I don't know how he does it."

Rhi's thoughts spun. "Then if you said it with the right intent, could you just kill someone? Just by speaking a name?"

"Hurt yes, to the point of death? No," replied the dragon.

"It needs a more physical action than that," said Shayne and then he added. "Are you planning on killing my brother?"

Before Rhi could respond, the dragon cut in.

"Yes! Of course!"

Shayne looked meaningfully at Rhi. She remembered his previous words to her.

"*It is never right to kill your own brother even if he has done everything to deserve it.*"

His gaze reminded her of these words.

Rhi frowned and hung her head as if she had been scolded.

"What's going on?" said the dragon, suspecting there had been a divergence of agreement. "You agreed you would help me kill him!"

Rhi sighed in frustration. "It's not that simple."

"What do you mean, it's not that simple? After you free me, I kill him. What could be simpler than that?" sputtered the dragon in confusion.

Here Shayne spoke up to defend her.

"He's not your brother, dragon. He's mine. I cannot condone murdering my sibling so lightly."

"Don't dragons have brothers and sisters?" Rhi had to interject.

There was a long silence from the dragon. "Yes," was the final answer.

"And what would you do if the tables were turned?" Shayne asked.

There came another long silence. "Dragon justice is very… complicated."

Rhi's eyebrows hopped. "Exactly!"

Rhi made a growling sound. "We have to give him a chance."

The dragon scoffed. "What sort of chance?"

Shayne nodded. "Yes, he must be given one last chance to redeem himself."

There came the sound of tumbling boulders. "And if he refuses, then can I kill him?"

Rhi looked at Shayne for permission. His face was clouded and dark as he thought.

Finally, after many minutes had passed, he nodded.

"Then I'm okay with it."

Rhi moaned and shook her head. "This means one more one-sided conversation with Nazar. Erg! How I hate these dinner dates with him!"

Shayne crept close to the bars, reached through and stroked her face gently. "You're being very brave. Hopefully this will all be over soon," he consoled.

She nodded without looking at him. "Yes, either we'll all be free or," here she paused and met his gaze. "Or I'll be a zombie and you'll be dead."

She swallowed with difficulty as tears sprang to her eyes. Shayne's hand squeezed her shoulder in encouragement.

"Shayne, I need to know one thing before the end."

He smiled easily. "Of course."

She closed her eyes and took a deep breath. And then she just blundered ahead with the words.

"If these could be my final hours...well the dragon and Nazar have both said...ugh! This is ridiculous! Shayne, do you love me?"

The last words had barely left her mouth when she felt the wall between them go up again. He removed his hand and his gaze from her face and physically withdrew a bit from her, back into the safety of his jail cell.

Rhi dropped her eyes and immediately regretted her words to him.

"What difference does it make?" he finally said to her. "I'm sure my brother has told you I'm a yellow-bellied coward. And he's absolutely right. I run away from everything, my responsibilities to my people and even my own feelings."

Rhi ground her teeth in frustration at his non-answer. "That was a long time ago. You've changed."

Shayne laughed a short, mean laugh. "Have I? You don't really know me. Who wants to be in love with a coward?"

Rhi grabbed the bars of the jail cell and pressed her face up against the cold metal. "The man who defended me from getting raped and killed by those robbers was no coward! Now answer the question!"

Her words forced him to look at her. He just stared at her for a long moment. Then he came back to sit beside her on the other side of the bars, reached through and held her face in both hands. He squeezed his eyes shut and pressed his forehead up against her own.

"Yes. From the minute I saw you I loved you although I didn't know why at the time. I have always loved you, *Mara*."

The dragon had been silent until now. Now it made a sudden, soft hiss. "So she *does* have a soul name after all! Interesting."

Rhi shuddered and felt tears spring to her eyes when he said the strange word. The mere utterance of the name caused a strange blend of emotions inside of her. She felt he had laid bare all her innermost secrets and yet, at the same time, she felt safe showing him her secret self, as if he could be trusted with anything she dared to tell him.

The dragon's voice rumbled above her. "And do you know his name?"

Rhi's thoughts whirled like dried leaves blown by an autumn wind.

"I..." she began but Shayne covered her mouth with his hand.

"Don't!" he warned her. "If you do know, don't speak it! Wait for the right time."

Rhi was afraid even to try to discover his name. If she knew of it, then Nazar might use it against her. She drove the thought of Shayne's soul name far away and tried to bury it deep. The curiosity of such a thing might well prove dangerous for everyone involved.

"The day grows old," she said with a difficult swallow. "And I have many things to say to Nazar tonight. I must plan out this conversation to come. My life might depend on it."

Shayne took hold of her hand and squeezed it tight. "Be careful," he whispered softly to her.

Rhi nodded, took a deep breath and forced herself to leave. She felt his eyes following her as she walked away. She forced herself not to look back.

CONSEQUENCES

Her thoughts were a million miles away as Rhi made her way back to her room. She requested a hot bath be drawn of the vacant eyed servant who met her at the doorway to her room. He silently nodded and left to do as she bid.

She thought hard as she bathed and brushed out her long locks. Then she plaited her hair into one long braid which hung down her back. She was still thinking. She requested a dress be laid out for her but a plain one this time. She returned in a robe to her room to find the requested clothing had been brought to her. There was a white tunic with a simple leather bodice and a plain green skirt laid out on the bed for her. It was perfect attire for a commoner.

It met with her satisfaction.

She dressed quickly and awaited the servant to appear at dusk and light her room.

She noticed the dragon return in the sky at dusk. Soon after, the servant appeared and lit the candles and the oil lamps in her room. Then a finely attired man-servant, one she had not seen before, entered her room.

The dragon had been silent until now.

"You will not be dining in the usual feast hall tonight. Nazar has planned the evening meal someplace else. Go with him, Rhi."

Rhi sniffed. "So it's tonight?"

"It would appear so."

Rhi took a deep, bracing breath. "Very well then. Let's get this over with."

She stood up and followed the servant obediently.

He led her through a maze of hallways she had never seen before to a smaller, more private table set on an open air stone porch positioned to offer a beautiful view of the valley below.

King Nazar stood there awaiting her. He was dressed in fine velvet and brocade gilded clothes and wore a bejeweled dagger at his hip.

Nazar looked her up and down and sniffed in disapproval of her simple attire.

Rhi dipped in a small curtsey.

"Sire," she said.

He said no greeting in return, just nodded in acknowledgement.

"Is there a reason for the change in dining areas, my Lord?" she asked.

He frowned darkly. "You have a decision to make tonight," he said flatly.

Calmly, Rhi nodded. "Yes, I do."

Her quiet manner and self-control seemed to surprise him somewhat.

"And?" he said. "What is your answer?"

"First I would like you to ask the question properly, my Lord." Rhi heard the dragon chuckling quietly in her mind.

Nazar sighed in exasperation. "Will you or will you not marry me?"

"Hmmm," murmured Rhi. Slowly she seated herself at the table. "Well, let us discuss marriage negotiations, shall we?"

Nazar's frown increased. "It is a simple question with a simple 'yes' or 'no' answer. What is there to negotiate?"

Rhi sipped her glass of wine slowly, taking her time in replying. "Quite a lot actually. But you, being a royal, should be used to all sorts of negotiations. So this should not be a big an issue. Be assured you will have a definite answer from me this night on this matter."

Having said this, she gestured to the chair across from her.

Nazar hesitated, then grudgingly, seated himself.

She considered him for a moment. "What if I would agree to marry you if certain requests were met?"

Her words took him aback for a moment. "That all depends on the nature of the requests. Which are?"

She took another sip of wine to steel herself and tried to act nonchalant. "First, I would like you to return your servants' souls to their bodies."

He smirked. "They would drop dead the second I did!"

Rhi made a guttural sound which warned him not to interrupt. "Second, I want you to free your dragon from its bondage to you."

She felt the dragon's hopes soar.

Nazar guffawed at this but Rhi held up her hand in a scolding manner.

"Third, I want you to release your brother from your dungeon."

There was a long silence as Nazar sat across from Rhi, staring at her as if he had just seen her for the first time.

Then he burst out in laughter.

"Are you mad?" he managed to choke out.

Rhi felt her hopes and the dragon's plummet.

"Those are the most ridiculous things I have ever heard! Why would I want to free my servants? Who would cook and clean for me? Do you expect me to do such things myself? And why would I free the dragon? It would kill me the moment I released it! And as for Shayne…"

Here he lapsed into an amused chuckling as he shook his head, thinking of such a prospect.

"Do you mistake me for an imbecile? I marry you and release him so you two can carry on behind my back? Do you really think I'm that foolish?"

His laughter suddenly stopped and he leant forward across the table towards her. He gently stroked the side of her face with a finger.

"Marry me Rhi and I promise you, when I do kill my brother, it will no longer matter so much to you."

Rhi withdrew her face from his touch with a look of utter disgust. "You're a horrible, cruel man!" she told him. "Why do you do these things to people? Why can't you just let them be?"

Nazar's face became hard and cold. "Because people make no sense at all. They say things which aren't true, they make promises they never keep, they change their minds. It should all be simple. But it's not simple. Except here. I make them simple."

He paused, considering her for a moment. "You see my dear, everyone lies. Every single person who walks this earth lies. You were lying to me the day you met me. But not here. These people don't lie. These people I'm able to understand. These people never hurt me. It's paradise here."

Rhi raised her chin in defiance. "Only for you!" she told him with some heat. "You can't judge people so quickly. Life is like rolling hills, lots of ups and downs. And people are...complicated. Situations in their lives change and that transforms the promises into lies. Situations they didn't plan on or they couldn't see happening. How can you blame people for that? It's out of their control. People are not meant to be simple. And you forcing them to be a way you can understand better is wrong. Nobody is happy here but you. Can't you see that?"

Nazar growled at her words. "You're wrong. It's different here. I control everything. Therefore I control the outcome of things."

Rhi shook her head. "You can't control everything, Nazar," she told him.

He sniffed in derision of her words. Then he waved a servant over and whispered something in his ear. The servant nodded and left. Nazar turned back to her.

"Oh no? I control everything in this kingdom, even you. Just watch me!"

His words made her shiver. Again she had lost her taste for food and drink. Her stomach lurched at the prospect of what unknown thing was to come.

"I know exactly how this will end. I know the decision you will make and how things will end up. I know the end of your story already and we're not even there yet. Would you like me to tell you?"

Rhi swallowed with difficulty. "I prefer to let my tale just play out."

He nodded and shrugged. "As you wish. It makes no difference to me."

Rhi heard the tread of boots behind her and turned around in her chair. What she saw made her gasp and jump to her feet.

Four blank faced soldiers were leading Shayne. His wrists were shackled with heavy iron manacles and his clothes were dirty from the dungeon. The soldiers pushed him forward and stepped back, ready and waiting.

"Ah! How nice of my brother to join us for dinner. Funny. He doesn't look as gaunt and starved as I expected him to be. I wonder why that is?" Nazar said in a mocking tone of voice.

"What are you up to, Nazar?" Rhi demanded.

King Nazar just smiled maliciously as he stood up and approached Shayne. Shayne stared straight ahead, refusing to look at his brother. For one breathless moment, Rhi thought Nazar had removed his soul like all the others. But a soul-less person had no need for manacles.

"Did you enjoy your life of freedom, o' brother of mine? Wandering the lands as if you had no responsibility or duty to anyone or anything? Was it fun living the life of a vagabond and a drifter?"

Shayne's eyes shifted to glare at Nazar but still he said nothing.

Nazar stepped closer to him, reached out and picked up the falcon's feather Shayne wore about his neck. Nazar studied it for a moment.

"But then you caught a pretty little bird, didn't you? One with a sharp beak and talons, but a pretty little falcon nonetheless."

A dangerous glint came into Shayne's eyes. "Leave her be, brother." he said. His tone was soft but his words hinted to the boiling emotions which lay beneath.

Nazar sniffed derisively at his younger, smaller sibling.

"Do I need to remind you I am king here? I will do what I wish, to whomever I wish."

Shayne gave a small pause to consider his reply before speaking it. "You are only the king of an empty land with soul-less servants. Who wants to be king of that?" said Shayne.

"At least I don't shirk my own responsibilities."

Nazar turned back to Rhi.

"So this is who you'd rather be with? A runaway and a coward? A wanderling prince with no plans for the future, no goals, no dreams? A beggar king? You prefer him to all I and this castle could provide you with?"

Rhi felt her face grow hot. She stepped up until she stood inches away from him.

"He was good to me and gave me my freedom. That is all I ever wanted," she told him. "Obviously you never bothered to learn what it is a woman wants. She cannot be wooed with fine dresses and jewels. Not if the heart behind it is black as coal. People are not so simple and love is *definitely* not simple!"

Shayne took a step forward. The soldiers did not move.

"Careful, Rhi…" he warned.

Nazar's eyes blazed down at her. "If you are to be my wife, you had better learn to mind your place."

His words made her blood boil. She didn't think about what she should say or do, she just reacted.

Rhi snarled and slapped him across the face as hard as she could.

Nazar stepped back, wide-eyed in shock. His hand went to his wounded cheek which was quickly turning red.

"Did you read that page of the story, Nazar? Did you see it coming?" she mocked him.

And then Nazar reacted. He growled in fury and the dagger at his hip was suddenly in his hand. Rhi heard Shayne shout something at her. And then he knocked her roughly out of the way, taking her place in front of Nazar. Rhi tumbled to the ground. As she did so she heard a meaty *thunk* behind her. She spun about and looked back towards the two brothers.

And then she began to scream.

The brothers were holding onto each other by the arms. The fancy, bejeweled hilt of Nazar's dagger was jutting out of Shayne's chest. He was staring at the hilt as if he recognized it.

"You didn't even bother to wipe Father's blood off..." Shayne said. His voice was soft and raspy.

And then he fell.

Rhi screamed his name and scrambled on her hands and knees over to Shayne. She caught his body before his head hit the marble. She turned him over in her arms and looked into his face.

But he was already gone.

She wept and rocked him, sobbing his name over and over again.

Softly in her mind, the dragon's voice spoke. *"Wanderling's choice, destiny's sacrifice."*

The dragon paused. "The sacrifice has been made. Now child, remember."

Rhi stilled her sobs as she forced her emotionally charged mind to think. She took a deep breath.

"Nazar, you do not know the end of this story." Her voice caught in her throat and she gasped.

"I'm tired of doing what everyone expects of me. This ends here and now. I will never marry you! And I am keeping my soul. You, however, have much to answer for."

She took the deepest breath she had ever done and, inclining her head back to the heavens, she screamed one name at the top of her voice.

"FIR'NAH MOCK!"

She felt the dragon roar in triumph in her brain as its soul rushed out of her body.

As the last syllables of the word faded, the rocks began to tremble. The trembling increased to a violent shaking of the land underneath the castle. Nazar was thrown to the stone floor.

"No!" he screamed. "You can't! It's not possible…"

The ground continued to heave and buck like a wild horse trying to toss its rider. The servants collapsed and lay still on the rocking floor. And then a rumbling snarl came from beneath the earth, turning into an enraged roar louder and greater than Rhi had ever heard before.

"You can't!" shouted Nazar. "What have you done? It will kill us all!"

Slowly Rhi turned her face about to look at him. "So?" was all she said. She no longer cared anymore about anything.

There was a sudden rush of wind on wings as the shape of the red, golden dragon hurtled up into the night sky before them. It spun about in mid-air and looked at the puny humans gathered beneath. Then its gaze focused on Nazar. The faceted rubies which were its eyes began to glitter like the flames of a wild fire. The dragon turned in its flight and aimed for the castle.

Nazar screamed in terror and turned to run. But the castle was still shaking and he was knocked roughly to the ground.

The dragon laughed in evil glee as it snatched Nazar up in midflight with one giant paw. Then it climbed high into the night sky carrying the screaming king. It hovered high in the air and tossed Nazar up above it like a dog playing with its ball. As he fell, the dragon aimed a bout of flames toward the falling human. He was incinerated in an instant. The charred remains fell into the cavernous maw of the dragon and were consumed.

Rhi turned her face away. She did not need to see any more. Nazar was dead. She was free.

A movement off to the side caught her eyes.

The servants were standing up and rubbing their faces. Their eyes were no longer blank and staring. They were slaves no more.

The ground had ceased to heave. Everything suddenly became very quiet.

The soldiers who had ushered in Shayne now came to her and knelt sympathetically by her side and bowed their heads in grief. Rhi looked about to see more servants filing into the area. The women fell to their knees and covered their faces. The men bowed their heads and knelt respectfully. No one spoke a word. It was so quiet and still. Only the torchlight buffeted by the wind moved.

And then a greater wind gusted and blew about them. The dragon had returned. It settled its great bulk on the edge of the rock wall. The servants stepped back and made room for it but they did not act the least bit frightened of the dragon. It was almost like he was simply a larger member of the throng gathered about her.

The dragon did not attack anyone. It bent its head low and peered closely at Rhi holding the dead body of Shayne. It sighed heavily and sadly.

"Now my dear, do you truly understand the meaning of sacrifice," the dragon said to her.

Rhi squeezed her eyes shut and the tears began again. "What are you doing here?"

The dragon cocked its head and looked at her curiously. "You spoke my soul name. I am now yours to command."

Rhi sighed and shook her head. "I want no one! No servant or slave to bow to me let alone a dragon! I spoke your name to free you. That was my only intent. You are free. Do as you wish."

The dragon considered her quietly for a moment. "No human has ever freed a captive dragon. It simply is not done. Everyone is too afraid of the consequences."

The dragon cocked its head to the other side. "I'm touched. I did not think it to be possible, that a human's action could move me. Therefore in freeing me, all you have done has been to make me indebted to you. You have still caged me with your sacrifice. I must repay the debt to rest easy."

But she shook her head in denial. "You have nothing I want," Rhi whispered.

The dragon chuckled. "I shared souls with you mere moments ago. I know what it is you want."

And here the dragon nudged Shayne's body gently with its snout.

Hope unlooked for leapt in her chest. "Can you bring him back to life?" she asked breathlessly.

The dragon smiled. "No. But I might be able to help *you* do that."

Rhi frowned. "I don't understand," she said.

"His soul is still here. It doesn't want to leave you. But it cannot return to its body. It won't accept the soul back with such a mortal wound. I can heal the body. You then can try to call him using his soul name. We will let Shayne decide whether he wants to return to life or not. Agreed?"

Rhi's heart began to pound again. She nodded frantically, not trusting her voice.

"Very well then. Remove the dagger and bare the wound for me. We need to work quickly before his body grows cold."

Two of the kneeling soldiers leaned forward to help. One withdrew the dagger, the other cut the tunic off of Shayne's body leaving his chest bare. A woman stepped forward with a bowl of water and some clean rags.

Rhi remembered the day she had spied on him bathing. She remembered the cold water glistening on his skin. His chest looked much different now with an ugly stab wound and blood pouring out all over.

A sob was torn from her. An old soldier took hold of her shoulders and squeezed them in encouragement.

"Good. Now stand back. This will only take a moment," the dragon instructed.

They gave the great reptile space.

The dragon bent its great red head, glistening with iridescent scales over the body of Shayne and breathed onto him. A mist like waves of heat issued out of the dragon's mouth onto the skin of Shayne's bare chest. Three times the dragon did this. Each time the wound grew smaller. The last time, the humans watched amazed as new skin and tissue knitted back over the horrible wound. In mere moments they wiped off the blood to find any evidence of an injury had disappeared. There wasn't even the hint of a small scar.

"Now," purred the dragon. "This is the moment he spoke of before. You need to call him back."

Rhi looked into the dragon's jewel-like eyes. She wasn't quite sure how this worked and she was a little afraid to try. She didn't know Shayne's soul name because she hadn't dared to try before and now she wasn't sure if she could even do it.

"Hurry child! The body grows cold," the dragon scolded her.

Rhi took a deep breath. She placed her hands on either side of his face and closing her eyes, she emptied her mind of all thoughts. She searched the emptiness for a sound which was his soul. Something tickled her thoughts, like the brushing of a bird's beating wings on skin. She spoke the something which touched her.

"Istay?" she whispered.

She felt the dragon's approval. Something stirred in her heart.

"Istay, come back to me," she said in a louder, more confident tone of voice. "I want you to come back. I'm not done knowing you yet. Please come back, Istay."

She felt something stir deep inside Shayne's form. She opened her eyes and looked at him. His death pale skin was fading, becoming more flush and rosy with life. His cooling skin was growing warm again.

Gently, Rhi placed his head on the marble and she laid an ear on his bare chest, listening for a heartbeat. Long moments passed with no sound, then there came the faintest of thumps. She bit her lip, afraid to hope. Another thumping sound followed, this time stronger and louder. Rhi smiled and a sob of relief was torn from her.

She felt his chest move. And then Shayne's arm lifted and gripped her in a strong embrace.

"I knew you were important," he said weakly. "I'm so happy it was you who saved me."

They sat up and embraced tightly.

"The king has returned," shouted one of the soldiers. "Long live the king!"

They were surrounded by the cheers of the people about them.

Shayne smiled. "I'm not the only thing that has returned," he said and pointed out to the valley below. The outline of a dark red horse silhouetted against the light of the full moon, stood on the nearest hilltop beneath them. It neighed and reared high up onto its hind legs.

Rhi was laughing and crying all at once.

"Falcon!"

⊖he open roao

Rhi stroked Falcon's glossy red side as she stood next to him and watched him take great swallows of water from the stream gurgling past them. The castle was miles behind them. It was a beautiful summer day. The sun was high in the sky and the clouds were scudding slowly by, blown by the wind from the mountains. It was a good day to travel.

Falcon lifted his head suddenly and looked back towards the castle, the direction they had come from. He nickered in greeting. He sensed another horse.

Rhi sighed heavily. She had been caught. Now she had to face the music.

She turned to look back and tried to steel herself for the conversation which was to come, a conversation she would much rather avoid.

A rider appeared galloping out of the shady darkness of the woods. He was mounted on a buckskin colored horse and was dressed in fine clothes. A royal blue cape fastened by a gold brooch on his shoulder, flapped in the speed of their passing. His straight blond hair flew back and there was a gold circlet on his brow.

It was Shayne wearing the attire of a king in office. He looked much different now the dungeons rags were off of him.

Rhi smiled as her eyes drank him in.

He pulled his blowing horse to a halt beside her, confusion marring his fine features.

"You look very fine. And you smell much better," she told him.

He ignored her words. "You're leaving?" he said.

Rhi hung her head and shrugged. "The road calls to me," was the only explanation she had for him.

Shayne shook his head. "You're leaving *me*," it was a statement this time with emphasis on the last word.

His tone of voice demanded an explanation.

Rhi heaved one heavy sigh. "I don't want to. You've done nothing to deserve this."

Shayne tilted his head as he looked down upon her. "Then don't leave. Stay with me. Please."

Rhi risked a look up at him through her long locks which had become tousled by the wind.

"There is nothing I'd like more," she said softly. "Look Shayne. I freed you and the people of your kingdom. And that was a very good thing. But you now have certain responsibilities and I..."

"You don't," he finished for her.

She smiled weakly and shrugged. "I am still just a farmer's daughter. And I am free now. I spent as much time as I wanted in that castle. I want...I *need*...to get back to the road. Can't you understand this?"

He was silent for a moment considering her words. "So this is goodbye, is it?" he said.

Rhi growled in frustration and ran a hand through her hair. "I don't want it to be. Shayne, I love you. But I can't ignore the road. And I can't expect you to drop everything you've won back to follow me. But I would like to know...if you could come with me...if it were possible...would you?"

It was his turn to utter a heavy sigh.

He dismounted his fine horse and dropped the reins so it could graze. He came up to her and wrapped her in the tightest embrace he could muster without crushing her.

"Oh, Rhiannon! There's nothing I want more than to drop every responsibility I have and become a wanderling again with you by my side. I wouldn't leave you with a pathetic note this time. I'd stay with you."

She nodded and squeezed her eyes shut against the tears which wanted to come. She returned his tight hug.

"But you're king now and you can't."

She felt him nod and then he stroked her hair. "That's right. I can't."

There was a long and very uncomfortable pause between them.

"May I at least ride for a little while beside you?" he asked her.

Rhi could not trust her voice to speak. She thought for just a moment to say no, but the moment passed quickly.

She nodded.

They remounted their horses and rode on. They talked about casual things. Conversation between them was stilted for each was thinking the same thing. But they never spoke of it to the other.

Shayne's mind was wildly racing all the while. He was trying to see how he could be king and wander with Rhi at the same time.

And then the dragon showed up.

It alighted ahead of them as they rode their horses through an abandoned field of wheat.

"What are you still doing here?" Rhi called out to him, laughing.

"Yes. I thought since she freed you, you would be off for dragon lands," Shayne added.

The dragon cocked its head at them and the sunlight flashed off of its shiny scales.

"I should," it replied. "But...well...I like it here. It's a very pretty kingdom with enough craggy rocks and mountains to make any dragon happy. I'd like to stay...with the king's permission of course."

A light suddenly dawned in Shayne's thoughts. A wild and crazy idea occurred to him.

"Maybe you can," Shayne said.

This time both Rhi and the dragon looked at him in confusion.

"Shayne, what are you up to?" Rhi said softly.

The dragon said nothing but its steady gaze at the new king mirrored Rhi's words.

Shayne thought desperately for a moment. The skeleton of a plan was forming in his brain. Yes, it just might work, he told himself.

"It's like this. My kingdom has sat stagnant and dormant for many years while Nazar insulated himself from the other kingdoms outside. Now I am on the throne, relations and trade must be reinstated. People who left in fear must be reassured all is well so they may feel they can safely return and take up their old lives again. But this will not happen without some work."

The dragon blinked. It followed his train of thought but was still confused as to where Shayne was going with this. Rhi's expression hinted the same.

"I and my lovely companion need to leave this realm to do this. We need to travel to the neighboring kingdoms to negotiate terms. We need to work at renewing old loyalties. We cannot do this from home. But we can also not leave the realm ungoverned and undefended."

Shayne looked at the dragon and smiled. "I am offering you the position of regent while I am away. Rule my kingdom in my absence until I return. Please do this for me, dragon. I offer you this position in my court. I do not force this job on you. You are free to refuse."

The dragon just stood there motionless and staring. Then it began to blink very quickly as it digested the information.

"You want me to be king in your stead?" the dragon said slowly.

"Yes!" said Rhi and Shayne at once.

The dragon blinked some more. "But...what will the people say?"

Rhi smiled and laughed a little. "If they were any other people and any other dragon, I would think they'd have quite a lot to say! But they aren't. They are people who suffered the same ill treatment as you. You both come from the same place emotionally. Would they trust any dragon? No, of course not. Would they trust you specifically? Yes!"

The dragon blinked a few more times and looked from Rhi to Shayne and back again.

"It is a temporary position, is it not? How long a time are we talking about here?"

Shayne replied. "We would go away and return may times."

The dragon muttered as it thought. "Many times meaning plural times, correct?"

"Summers you would rule while we were away and winters we would return," Rhi said.

"You would be free to stay the winters if you like," added Shayne.

"Hmmm," muttered the dragon considering. "Give me a moment to think about this."

As the dragon said this, it sprang into the air and they watched as it climbed high into the afternoon sky. After becoming a tiny red speck in the blue, they watched as it circle an area of sky. It circled several times and then folded its wings and came plummeting back to earth. Just before it seemed the beast would crash into the ground, it spread its wings and landed as lightly as a sparrow.

"I think better when flying," it explained.

"Well? What is your answer?" Rhi said breathlessly.

The dragon bowed low to the Shayne. "I humbly accept the appointment of regent of the realm. I will endeavor to rule your kingdom with wisdom, justice and fairness in all manners pertaining to the post of office you have laid at my feet. And when you return, I will calmly and willingly relinquish my duties to the proper lord and king of the realm."

Shayne smiled. "I am so happy you accepted."

The dragon looked up and winked smugly at the both of them. "I bet you are! Now you two can run off together and have more adventures! You truly are wanderlings at heart."

Rhi beamed at them both. "May your rule be peaceful until we return, dragon."

The dragon bowed its head. "And may the road before you be smooth. May your adventures be just exciting enough to give your life zest but not so perilous it puts your lives in jeopardy. Travel far, come back soon and in one piece."

Shayne looked at Rhi. She was beaming at him. She sidestepped Falcon closer to his horse and leaning halfway out of the saddle, planted a passionate kiss on his mouth.

The dragon made a sound of disgust. "Must you do that in front of me? Blech! Human relations are so…sloppy!"

But they only laughed at his reaction.

Shayne and Rhi turned their horses about and took their leave of the dragon. They left the realm and traveled onwards together and free.

The End

Other Works by This Author

DEADLY CONVERSATIONS